Ghosts of the Past

Ty Eros

This fictional work is purely from the heart, mind, and soul of the author and any similarities to actual persons or situations are completely coincidental.

ISBN: 0692547290
ISBN-13: 978-0692547298

DEDICATION

This book is for every person that's ever been lost in the storm of their own mind. The mistakes of your past should not be shackles that bind you but allow them to be stepping stones to a better you. Learn from each moment of trial and adversity and claim your victory at every turn.

CONTENTS

ACKNOWLEDGMENTS

As always I want to thank all of my supporters! Those who have been there with me since day one and even those who just met me. Mokha Kentwood I love you big bro, you've been by my side since day one and have been somewhat of a mentor. I doubt I would have really gotten the first book published if you weren't there for me to bug lol. Lastly, but most importantly I got to thank the fans, all my Facebook friends, followers on Instagram and twitter, you all have been such a tremendous help to me!

CHAPTER 1: COLD FEET

It had been ten years since I'd seen my high school buddies Derrick and Lisa. Ten years since I made the decision to take a new job, move to DC, and make a new life for myself. I can remember it like yesterday, that faithful day of bittersweet bliss. It was the day when I laid my parents to rest forever and celebrated the triumph of receiving my master's in public health. It was a welcome uplift to the sorrow of the morning and after the tragic loss of my both my parents in a car accident just weeks before. It was also later that same night that my best friend Derrick and his fiancée, Lisa, rejoiced over the arrival of my godson DJ. Someone who I'd been watching grow up through pictures, text

1

messages, and phone calls. Since I'd been away I still did my share of spoiling him with money and gifts, however, I knew that wasn't enough. If you let some other folk tell it I never should have left or you might just hear people say that I was a coward for leaving. Even my aunt and ex-wife, who knew the truth, were contributors to the lies and vicious rumors that floated around. Now truthfully maybe things could have been handled differently, but this job I have now conveniently came around at the right time. Not to mention at the time I was morning my parents, freshly divorced, and a twenty-five year old college graduate with a rising career. I would have been foolish to let the bullshit in my personal life stop me from getting what I'd worked my ass off for over the last seven years. Nevertheless, in less than ten hours I would be boarding a flight headed to "happy valley" aka my hometown of Violet, LA. Though I was excited to see my friends I wasn't anticipating seeing others or dealing with the drama that I knew my return would bring. Yet at this point it was too late for me to change my mind. So I laid there in my bed wrestling with my pillows as I restlessly contemplated the best way to deal with the imminent stress.

Finally morning came, and after getting less than five hours of sleep I took my shower, brushed my teeth, got dressed, and made my way to the airport. Still having my reservations I made it up in my mind that I would do my best to enjoy this trip. Derrick was gonna pick me up from the airport and bring me to my parents' house where I would be staying. The thought of seeing that six foot two, muscle bound piece of dark chocolate with the golden smile sort of put my mind at ease. When I got to my seat I reminisced about how he used to eat my ass in the basement after school when we were teenagers. I would of course reciprocate and suck his dick and sometimes he would fuck me or vice versa, but I was almost sure none of that was gonna be happening now. Though I did miss our sessions, he was married with two kids now, one of which was DJ my godson. I looked out at the clouds as we ascended into the sky and began to relax as I replayed our rendezvous in my mind.

"Excuse me sir would you like a soda or cocktail," the flight attendant asked.

"Sure, Jack and Coke would be great," I replied, turning to see a pretty young lady with beautiful, full lips and nice, perky breast.

"Sure I'll get that to you right away," she stated.

"And make it as strong as possible," I added as she walked away.

A few moments later she returned with my drink and some nuts. I immediately started gulping it down and then I noticed something was written on the napkin she'd given me. I started to just ball it up figuring it was just a phone number but I decided that since she took her time to write it, and she took care of me with the drink, it was worth reading. So I opened it up and read, "Meet me in the bathroom when the light goes off." I laughed to myself and stuffed it in my pocket before reclining in my seat again.

"Shawty must like what she see," I said to myself.

"Attention passengers," a cheerful male voice came over the speaker, "My name is Kyle Dawson and I'll be your pilot today! First of all I want thank you for choosing DPS Airlines and I hope that you enjoy your flight. I won't bore you with all the technical stuff, but in the event that there is an emergency please remain calm and listen carefully to any and all instructions given by myself or the flight attendants. If you should need anything during the trip, feel free to call on our attendants Tina and Jasmine and they will be glad to assist you. Once again, thank you for flying with us and enjoy the flight!"

At the conclusion of his speech I noticed the fasten seatbelt light had gone off so I unbuckled and looked around for the attendant. I was sort of apprehensive about it but those lips and breast had caught my attention. I slowly made my way to the back of the plane taking a mental inventory of all the sexy muthafuckas that were on board.

"Hey can I help you," the other flight attendant asked, rising from her seat.

"Uh, I was actually just looking for the bathroom," I answered, "I've been having to piss since I got on," I added, playfully fondling my dick and prancing as I spoke.

"Oh ok, it's straight back on your left right in front of the coach doors," she replied paying no mind to my gesture.

I proceeded on back as she instructed and entered into the door that said vacant. Once inside I locked the door to activate the occupied light. In my mind a million thoughts were swimming around. I never thought of myself as being real attractive or sexy, but since I been hitting the gym more regularly I've been getting a lot more attention. At 5'11 and 223lbs I was always kind of cocky but my body was never really all that defined. I stood there in the mirror on the back of the door and admired the progress I was seeing. Most times when people asked me what my best features were I would say my eyes or my smile. My ex-wife used to say she loved my ass and the thick, 9.5in caramel pipe also known as my dick. I began to lose myself in thought as I stood there but then I heard a light tapping on the door. Figuring it had to be the attendant I went ahead and opened it.

CHAPTER 2: MILE HIGH CLUB

"I didn't know if you would come or not," she said as she entered, "I've honestly never done this before but it's been a long time for me and when I saw you I decided to take a chance. I hope I don't seem like a hoe or nothing," she began to babble.

"It's cool, I've never been invited into an airplane bathroom before either and I honestly didn't know what to expect when I came back here. Even though I did have an idea of what it could've been," I replied.

"Well, I guess that makes us both amateurs huh," she laughed.

"Yea I guess so shawty, so wassup," I inquired.

"You might think I'm crazy but I really just want to see your body and maybe I'll do you a favor too. I've been admiring your chest and arms since you got on this morning, and my name is Tina by the way," she said.

"You want to see my body," I laughed.

"Yes, do you mind taking your shirt off," she urged.

"What the hell, I don't care," I laughed, as I peeled off my t-shirt.

"Oh wow, you must live in the gym," Tina cried, running her hand across my chest as she admired my body.

"I try to get there at least four times a week, but I'm still working on getting things tighter," I said, blushing from the attention.

"That's sexy too," she laughed.

"What is?" I asked.

"You're blushing, I hope I'm not

making you uncomfortable or embarrassing you," she said nervously, pulling her hands away.

"No you're good, and Deshawn is my name, but friends call me Shawn" I replied, placing her hands back on my chest and pulling her closer to me, "So you like what you see so far," I asked, sliding my hands around her waist.

"It's perfect, now I guess I need to show you something," Tina stated, pulling back a little, removing her vest, and unbuttoning her blouse.

"You sure this is ok, I don't want to get you in any trouble," I asked, "I mean what if there's cameras in here," I added.

"Trust me, everything is fine," she answered seductively as her eyes invited me to feel her breast, "Jasmine can handle the passengers for a while, and most are sleeping by now anyway," she continued.

"Ok..." I agreed hesitantly, "Damn...these are nice, real nice," I gasped,

taking hold of the plump, perfectly round c-cups that caught my attention when she first approached me.

"Maybe you should get a closer look," Tina suggested, opening the clasp on the front of her bra and gently guiding my face closer to her chest.

At that point all the introductions had been made and intentions were noted so no further conversation was needed. Like a newborn baby I instinctively took her breast into my mouth, hungrily sucking, licking, and nibbling on her nipples. She moaned receptively, digging her nails into my arm, and bitting her bottom lip as she stared lasciviously into my eyes. I took this a cue to take things a little further and slipped my hand under her skirt. Though it was a few inches away from my fingertips I could tell that pussy was getting wet as I squeezed her ass. If I had known that I'd get this kind of treatment on the flight last night I might not have been so apprehensive about it. Hell I might have even been excited about it, well this part of the trip at least. As hard as I tried to resist the moist warmth emanating from between her legs drew me in. I slid my finger under the rim of her panties and into her pussy. It was just as wet and warm as I imagined it would be, begging me to explore it deeper. Releasing a high pitch cry, Tina clinched tighter to my arm as I slipped in a second finger and worked them around inside her. Moments later her free hand found my dick, grasping it firmly through my sweats while I began to massage her clit. The next few moments were a blur and before either of us knew or could explain it one of her legs was wrapped around my arm, panties pulled aside, and my dick was balls deep inside her. Just then there was a tap on the door followed by a female voice.

"Girl I hope yall almost most done in there because we bout to land and the feds gon be checking the plane so I need you out here ASAP," she warned.

"Oh shit, that's Jasmine, I don't want to but I got to go baby," Tina moaned reluctantly.

"It's cool, I'll see you when we land right?" I asked as I pulled out.

"Yea, I'll be in New Orleans till tomorrow morning if nothing changes between now and then," she answered, dropping to her knees and taking my dick into her mouth.

"Whoa shit... what... you doing... I thought you had to go," I stammered from the sensation of her hot mouth on my dick.

"I do but not till I get all my pussy off this dick and taste your cum," she hissed lustfully.

"Mumm fuck... get that shit then shawty," I groaned.

About an hour and forty-five minutes later we were back in the air and on our way, once again, to our destination. Apparently the FBI got a tip that there was someone on the plane with a bomb. Fortunately it turned out to be a hoax but two people were taken into custody on outstanding warrants. Tina and I exchanged looks as she would pass though the aisle periodically, but no words were spoken. Maybe she felt guilty about letting me fuck her in the bathroom or maybe I had just been used to fulfill a sex addict's craving for sex. Either way, I got to bust a nice ass nut on those gorgeous breasts and in her mouth. From the looks of things it seemed like we would be landing in the city in another hour or so, so I decided to get a nap in before we did. However, that nap didn't last long, about twenty minutes in we met some rather rough turbulence that woke me. So I just laid there looking out the window and trying to go back to sleep.

"Shawn, are you sleep," Tina asked, dropping down in the seat next to me.

"Nah the turbulence woke me up, wassup?" I replied.

"Yea it kind of dis

turbed a lot of people, but I see most of yall up here are still sleeping or just not too concerned. I wanted to tell you I enjoyed this though," she said, boldly grabbing my dick as if no one was sitting across the aisle.

"You wild ma," I laughed.

"I'm serious, I want some more," she said, scooting closer to me.

"Shit you keep playing with it like that I might just have to give it to you," I joked.

"Maybe you should then," she replied, giving me that same look as she did earlier.

"Why don't you sit on my lap for a sec," I suggested, thinking she would probably object.

"Let me get you hard first, then sit on your lap," Tina countered, this time slipping her hand into my sweats and pulling my dick out through my boxers.

"That sounds interesting, but ain't you scared somebody gon see," I said, attempting to cover myself.

"No, they all sleep remember," she reiterated.

"Somebody could wake up though," I laughed.

"Boy stop acting all scared ain't nobody gon see nothing, here you play with this," she said, placing my hand between her legs, "While I play with this," she continued, stroking my dick to life once again.

"Damn that pussy wet as fuck shawty," I said, dipping my fingers into the pot for the second time.

"This dick... tastes good too," she exclaimed between the swirls of her tongue around the head of my dick.

"Shit, if yall take care of folk in first class like this I need to fly with DPS all the time," I moaned as she took my semi hard dick into her hot mouth.

"I don't know about any other passengers, but I'll definitely take good care of you anytime you're with me," Tina stated.

"Humm... you sure I'm the first passenger you've done this with? You seem real confident about what you want and how you want it now," I said.

"Not the first passenger I've fucked, but you're definitely the first one I've messed around with in the air," she replied, rising up and straddling my lap.

"Guess that means we've been initiated into the mile high club huh," I laughed.

"Humm I guess so," she stated, slowly allowing my dick to penetrate her gate again.

"Ok... oh... damn you riding that dick good shawty," I moaned in response.

"That's my intention daddy," she moaned back, going all the way down and up again on my dick while slowly winding her hips in a circle.

CHAPTER 3: MY NIGGA, MY NIGGA

I laid back and allowed Tina to ride my dick till we both came. Then after a quick wipe down she was gone again and I drifted off to sleep. There were a few times when the volume of our moans escalated to disturbing levels but luckily no one woke up. I think that made me cum harder though. The danger of being caught added a strange excitement to our public rendezvous. I can't quite remember how long I was asleep, but it was damn sure a good ass nap. Being awakened by the other attendant, Jasmine, I realized that I'd slept through the rest of the flight. So I quickly gathered myself, grabbed my bag from the overhead compartment, and made my way off the plane to the baggage claim area where I was met by Derrick. Once in the truck I couldn't help but notice how much sexier he'd gotten in the last ten years. The recent video calls were all mostly just from the neck up so I never saw the full body, but I can tell you it was no disappointment. I'm sure Tina would love to get her hands on him if she could.

"My nigga, my nigga my muthafuckin nigga, I can't believe you're really here," Derrick cried in excitement.

"Me either, but I am," I replied with a forced smile.

"I know man, but I'm definitely glad to see you and I know Lisa and DJ will be glad to see you as well. Shit last time you saw DJ he was a baby, so I'm sure he'll be glad to put a face with the all the gifts and voice he's been hearing all these years," he reasoned.

"Yea I guess you're right about that, but I know there's some other people who won't be so glad about my return," I said.

"Maybe so, but let's not worry about

that now. Most of them think you aren't coming till Sunday morning so we have two days to enjoy before you even have to think about running into any of them," Derrick assured me.

"Humm, I'm sure you and Lisa had something to do with that," I laughed.

"You know we did," he confessed, flashing that classic D-Roc smile at me.

"Oh yeah I knew it nigga, but yo can we pass by the graveyard? I'd like to visit my parents," I asked nervously.

"Are you sure you're up for that," Derrick inquired.

"Yeah bro, I'm good, not to mention you're coming with me," I answered.

"Oh ok, just make me the tag-a-long while you set yourself up for an emotional crisis," he joked, smiling at me once again.

"You'll be fine, and why you keep smiling at me like that nigga," I exclaimed, playfully punching him on the arm.

"Cause I miss you nigga, and you've gotten kind of sexy over the years. Chest and arms getting all toned and big," he said, reaching over and squeezing my chest.

"Aight nigga, stop that touchy feely shit, and watch the road," I snapped, pretending not to like the attention.

"Stop fronting nigga," Derrick said, seeing through my act and paying me no mind and continuing to feel me up.

"Ok two can play this game nigga," I replied, reaching into his lap and feeling for my old, one-eyed friend.

"Say bruh chill out," Derrick cried, swiping my hand away from his lap.

"Oh so it's all good for you to feel on me but I can't feel on you," I said with a smirk, sliding my hand back over his thigh, this time striking gold.

"Come on Shawn you know that ain't how I... you better stop before you get yo ass in trouble nigga," he warned, licking his lips

and turning his attention to the road.

"Maybe a little trouble is what I want," I replied tightening my grip on his hardening dick.

"Fuck man, you know I haven't fucked with a dude since you left, and I definitely don't want DJ to know his daddy fucks niggas," Derrick said, slowly giving in to my ploy.

"Lisa never knew till we decided to tell her and it's been ten years since I've had this pipe inside me," I stated, selfishly ignoring his concern for his family.

"She did have her suspicions though, and us telling her only confirmed what she had already been thinking," he answered, "Plus she's expecting us now, I'm actually surprised she hasn't called to see where we are yet," he added.

"If she calls we can just explain to her that my flight was delayed due to the FBI bringing the plane down for a bomb search, which is what really happened so you

wouldn't be lying to her. She also knows that you're with me, your best friend that you haven't seen in ten years," I reasoned, finally succeeding at freeing Derrick's dick from his pants.

"Wait, what you mean a bomb search?" Derrick cried.

"Don't get excited, it was a false alarm but they did take some people in for unrelated stuff," I said, calming him down before the thought of anything else negative would have the chance to inundate his mind.

"But... they... shit nigga..." he stammered, feeling the head of his dick being probed by my tongue before being completely engulfed in my mouth.

"Don't worry about it just keep your eyes on the road my nigga," I instructed, skillfully taking that chocolate lollipop down into the back of my throat.

"Fuck... shit ok nigga," Derrick moaned helplessly, placing his free hand on top of my head, "Damn you really ain't playing with

that shit huh nigga, let me feel that ass yo," he
added.

"I told you I missed this shit nigga," I
*answered quickly, repositioning myself so he
could get what he requested.*

*"Shit I'm a have to pull over for a
minute bruh," Derrick growled, smacking my
ass.*

*About ten minutes later we had pulled
into the parking lot of what looked like an
abandoned warehouse. Derrick was
aggressively fucking my throat like it was a
pussy and I was loving that shit, not to
mention he also had two fingers in my ass.
The sound of cars passing on the highway
only added to the excitement, knowing that
someone could pull in the parking lot and
catch us. Thankfully the truck glasses had
dark tint, but that wouldn't stop the "Good
Samaritan" or some curious person from
knocking on the window. Derrick's hedonistic
grunts probably wouldn't have left much to
the imagination though.*

"Aye nigga I didn't expect all this but I

got to feel that ass now son," Derrick cried with bated breath.

"I know you didn't think I was gon be gone for ten years and just forget about this dick huh," I laughed, waving his own dick at him before gulping it down again.

"Shit... the thought crossed my mind that we might do something, but I didn't think you would hop off the plane and onto my dick," he stated, fighting to hold back what he was feeling.

"Well it wasn't planned, and to be honest I got it in twice during the flight. Yo ass just started feeling on a nigga and I couldn't resist wanting to feel on you back," I said releasing his pulsing pipe just before it was ready to fire.

"Well let's hold off for a second and finish this when I get you to your house. This is hot but I want the reunion sex to be right," he said, "And nigga I got yo feel on you back, but let's get the hell out of here," he added jokingly, the phone ringing just as he got the words out.

"Let me guess," I laughed.

"You already know," Derrick replied, "Hey babe we're getting on the interstate now," he chirped, answering the call, "Shawn is great, you won't believe how good... Yea we're just gonna stop at the graveyard and we'll be on the way to the house... Aight love we'll see you in a bit," Derrick stated, concluding the seemingly one sided conversation, "Lisa just told me that your delay made the news bruh," he added.

"So she already knew we would be late," I replied.

"Yea, man it seems like the older she gets the more she knows about everything," he laughed.

"Nah it ain't that she's getting smarter y'all have just been together so long that she knows you better than you think. Lisa is paying more attention to things and you're getting lazy son," I joked.

"So you think she'll know you sucked my dick nigga," he asked with a slight smile

while his eyes cried with worry.

"Dude, if it worries you that much I'll tell Lisa I did and then ask her if it's ok if her husband fucks his best friend a few times while he's in town," I replied sarcastically.

"Nigga you trying to be funny but I'm a tear that ass up when I get you alone again," he snapped.

"Is that supposed to be a threat? I want you to dick me down nigga," I laughed.

"Ok go head and laugh now, you ain't gon be laughing Sunday when I'm pistol whipping that ass. You gon be begging for mercy nigga," Derrick exclaimed, smiling arrogantly.

"Yea I bet nigga, put your dick where you mouth need to be and show me! Better yet you can put my dick where your mouth is son," I stated, laughing even harder.

"Bet you'd like that huh," he replied.

"You already know I love getting my dick sucked and I especially love getting my

ass ate," I retorted.

"Aight keep talking, we gon see what happens when we get to that house," he said sternly.

CHAPTER 4: AWAKING THE DEAD

Fifteen minutes later we pulled up at the graveyard where my parents had been laid to rest. I did my best to hold it together, but about halfway to their graves all the pain and emotion of the day came rushing back to me. Fortunately Derrick was there by my side to help me push through. I think if he hadn't been there I may have just broken down in the middle of field or turned back. In my mind the mental blocks that I thought I had fortified by making a success of myself broke like damns as I stood face to face with my parents' tomb. Those few solemn moments felt like hours as I wept in Derrick's arms. There was comfort in the fortress of his compassion, but reality was harsh in reminding me of what secrets lay in my past. Knowing that I never got the chance to tell my parents how much I appreciated them. My heart bled at the fact that my last words to them were grossly impudent. A mere expression of their contempt for my lifestyle choices led to an argument that would never be resolved. I was bi and proud of it but the fact that it contributed to the end of my marriage disgusted them. Not to mention that my Aunt Penny was telling everybody all sorts of bullshit about how I had been caught fucking one of my professors. Then there was the other lie that I had caught numerous STD's and gave them to Tyra, my ex-wife. Lastly was the rumor that I was sucking dick to get grades, also the spawn of my ex's spite for me. Nobody acknowledged the fact that she was the one I caught with the two high school boys that were supposed to be helping with the yard work. It seemed like it was easier for people to believe the juicy rumors rather than the truth. Honestly, Tyra knew all about my sexuality when we meet, but when it seemed convenient she turned that shit on me. What pissed me off wasn't the fact that she attempted to out me but she challenged my intelligence and integrity bringing disgrace to my family name, thusly, causing the argument between my parents and me. Still, even though I was mad, they were mad, and some things were said that shouldn't have been I loved my parents with every ounce of my being. So in those moments standing there at their grave I yearned for the chance to take all those hatful remarks back. I wished that they could have seen how much I had accomplished. I consoled myself with the imaginative notion that they were watching and smiling down on me from heaven.

"Hey man, are you ready to go," Derrick inquired, noticing the mental torture I was putting myself through.

"Not yet, I just want to have a few more moments with them. You can go on to the truck, I'll be ready soon," I replied.

"Ok bruh, but if you take too long I'm coming get you. I know you feeling some kind of way about what happened, but I know Mrs. Gina and Mr. Daniel would be proud of you if

they could see you now," he said.

"Yea I'm sure they'd be real proud of their sexually confused, freeloading son," I retorted, recalling the words of my father.

"They loved you dude, regardless of what people said about you or what may have been thought you were the jewel of their affections," he countered.

"I bet they did, but it sure didn't feel like love when my heart was being ripped to shreds," I groaned.

"Love isn't always expressed with roses my dude. Sometimes our passion can be confused as spite when we only want the best for those we love, but I'll leave you alone man. If you need me just call," Derrick retreated, leaving a few words of wisdom.

"I'm sorry I caused so much pain," I sobbed softly once I was alone, "If I had the chance I'd take every ache of your hearts and turn it into joy. If only you could see me now! I may not be the family man as planned, but I've got two degrees, I'm making over 100k a

year. Dad I even drive a have black Bentley that I hand wash and polish in your honor, and mom I know you'd love the house I brought. I've got some beautiful white roses that remind me of the strength and grace you possessed and passed to me. I just wish you both could be here to feel how much I love you! I want to show you that I'm not a disappointment and let you know that I wasn't a wasted investment of your time, money, love, and support," I shouted, dropping to my knees crying profusely, "I'm not a confused hoe disgracing your name..."

"Come on dude let's get out of here," Derrick suggested, literally picking me up by my waist and walking me back to the truck, "Deshawn I never told you this but I'm more than proud of who you are son. It hurts me that you had to leave to make it, but fate has a way of making things work in our favor. I hate to see you beat yourself up like that, but I'm glad too that you're getting those feelings out. Just know bruh that I love you with all I got and nothing will change that son. You're like the brother I never had and I look up to you

nigga. Now come over here and let me dry those tears," he continued once we were in the truck. Pulling me close and wiping my face with his shirt before kissing my forehead and starting the engine.

CHAPTER 5: IT'S PADRINO!

A little over thirty minutes later we were pulling into Derrick's driveway. The ride there had been fairly quiet with the exception of the radio playing. After either hearing or seeing us DJ came flying out the door and nearly knocked me over while tackling me with affection before I could even take a step towards the house. It was a welcome that I was more than happy to receive. Especially after my emotional breakdown at the graveyard, being embraced by my godson made my day. Derrick grabbed my bags out of the trunk and somehow I managed to wobble to the door with DJ glued to my hip. Lisa met us there looking like she hadn't aged at all over the past ten years. Looking at her it was no wonder Derrick was a little resistant to play. Hell if I had a diamond like Lisa on my arm I wouldn't have need for a side gig either. DJ was a reward as well, strong, healthy, intelligent, and good looking just like his three parents. Sorry I had to put myself in the mix, I did contribute after all.

"Son why don't you let Padrino go so he can get in the house, then you can show him your surprise," Derrick said sternly.

"Are you staying with us Padrino," DJ asked innocently, looking up at me with his adorable eyes.

"Yes and if you're good your daddy and I will take you to get some pizza and ice cream," I answered.

"Woo hoo, yay," DJ exclaimed as he ran off.

"Pizza and ice cream, really Shawn? After I just had a long discussion with him about why he needs to eat the vegetables I cooked," Lisa scolded, rolling her eyes at me.

"Baby he ain't know what you had cooked," Derrick reasoned.

"Oh no I knew broccoli or some kind of sulfuric vegetable was cooking when I got to the door. So I know my godchild is gon need something fun to wipe away the trauma of that experience," I laughed.

"You know what Deshawn Anthony St. Julian you can take yo ass back to DC," Lisa retorted.

"Awww come on babe you know I'm just messing with you, come here and give me a hug girl," I empathized sarcastically, pulling her into my arms.

"Nigga just cause you done got a lil buff these days don't mean you can be grabbing all up on me," she squawked trying to wiggle away from me.

"I can remember when you used to be all over me. Don't act like you don't like me now," I said, holding tighter to her petit, curvy frame.

"Derrick you just gon stand there and let this gringo molest me," Lisa shrieked, almost instantaneously followed by another high pitched squeal coming from upstairs, "Now y'all done woke up that damn girl! I'm a deal with y'all asses once I get her settled," she snapped, jerking away and punching me in the chest.

"Nigga you know she gon fuck you up later, but them was some hot sessions between the three of us son," Derrick stated.

"Now you want to reminisce about..."

"Padrino, Padrino come see my new computer, I want to show you this new game I've been playing," DJ yelled excitedly from the stairs, cutting me off.

"I thought you were going get Padrino his surprise son," Derrick shouted back.

"Oh yea I forgot, I'm coming right back," DJ cried.

"Just meet us down in the basement with it son, and stop all that running in the

*house, I'm going take Padrino to his room,"
Derrick replied sternly.*

"Ok, ok," DJ reiterated.

*"I think you'll really like the lil
surprise DJ got you, I don't know how often
you'll use it but I'm sure you'll like it,"
Derrick said, turning his attention to me.*

*"Well if my godson thought enough of
me to get me something I'll do my best to
make use of it as much as possible," I replied.*

*"I hear you bruh, come on and follow
me to this room," Derrick laughed, grabbing
my suitcase and making his way towards the
kitchen.*

*"Why you laughing nigga," I inquired
as I picked up my other bag and followed.*

*"Oh no reason bruh, I just know you
that's all," he answered.*

"What that mean," I retorted.

*"Just what I said bruh, I know you and
if yo ass don't really like something,*

regardless of who gave it to you, yo ass is not gon use it," Derrick stated.

"Yea ok, I guess, what that woman cooked to go with the broccoli," I asked changing the subject.

"Ugh... arroz con pollo? I think that's how you say it," he replied, "We've done some renovating in the past year and this is one of the bathrooms down here and there's an on suite in the room where you'll be. We also added a media room and redid the laundry, but this will be your room. We made sort of an in-law suite down here," he added as he opened the door to the room.

"Wow, yall been doing some work huh, this shit is nice bruh. Last time I saw this place was in a picture and it was far from this, shit I actually started to get a lil worried when you said you were taking me to the basement," I laughed.

"You should know we wouldn't fuck over you like that bruh," he said.

"True, but ugh... Lisa looking sexy as

hell bruh, you think she'll let me hit that before I leave," I asked, casually grabbing my nuts and grinning deviously.

"Nigga did you just ask if you could fuck my wife," Derrick asked, looking at me like I had gone crazy.

"I did but I was only kidding bruh, don't have a baby nigga," I answered, arrogantly staring back at him.

"Don't get cocky nigga, and..."

"Dad... Padrino..." DJ called announcing his presence in the basement and cutting Derrick off.

"We're in the bedroom son," Derrick replied, still eyeing me down.

"Nigga if you want some come get it," I taunted, dropping down on the queen sized bed that was neatly made up.

"Don't worry I'm a get that ass, and when I tell Lisa what you said she gon tag it too," he replied.

"Here, I brought this for you Padrino, well Mom and Dad gave me the money and helped me pick it, but it's ok cause I'll have a job like you one day and I'll buy you something real, real nice," DJ stated proudly as he reached me the rectangular shaped box that was surprisingly kind of heavy.

"Ha, ha thanks lil man, why don't you help me open it," I suggested, taking it from him and placing it on the bed beside me.

"Ok!" he exclaimed, jumping into my lap, "Dad you can help too," he added with excitement.

"Ok son, but I'm sure you and Padrino are strong enough to handle it yourselves. I'll just sit here and watch in case you need me," Derrick laughed as he sat next to me.

"Oh wow, you got this for me," I exclaimed, lifting the Louis Vuitton bag out of the box.

"Yep, look inside Padrino," DJ chirped, anxiously pulling at it.

"Ok, ok give him a second son," Derrick scolded.

"Sorry," DJ moaned remorsefully.

"It's ok DJ," I said, rolling my eyes at Derrick while I opened the bag.

"Don't even go there Shawn," he snapped at me.

"Nigga are you serious," I cried, pulling out the contents of the bag.

"You like it Padrino," DJ asked innocently.

"I love it man, thank you," I replied tightly embracing him.

"Oh yea!" DJ cheered, bouncing up from my lap, *"I'm going tell my mom you liked it! It was her idea to get you the cologne so you can smell nice,"* he added.

"Ok son, go on back upstairs so I can talk to Padrino for a minute," Derrick instructed him.

"Ok, he likes it, he likes it, Padrino,

Padrino likes it," DJ sang happily as he went
bouncing out of the room.

*"Derrick, yall ain't have to buy me all
this stuff, I mean you already know I love me
some Louie, but I know it's..."*

*"Don't even say it and trust me bruh if
it was gon break the bank we wouldn't have
went anywhere near that store, plus we have
another surprise for you later after we get the
kids settled in bed,"* Derrick said, cutting me
off.

"Another surprise? For me?" I
repeated curiously.

*"Yea and it was her idea too, but you
got to wait till later, I wasn't even supposed to
tell you that but you know I'm horrible at
keeping secrets,"* he laughed.

*"Well go head and tell me what it is
then,"* I encouraged.

*"Nah you ain't bout to get me caught
up like that my nigga,"* Derrick laughed
again, laying back on the bed.

"But anyway I thought that you were supposed to be mad with me," I inquired.

"Nah I was just fucking with you, we used to fuck her together so I can't be mad if you want to taste it again," he said.

"Aight, aight I feel you, but you know things might have changed since yall got married. I got it though and I ain't gon twist your arm, but can I at least get another taste of you before we eat. Since we're alone and all I'm just saying," I said as I ran my hand up his thigh.

"I was actually thinking the same thing bruh, I guess after ten years we still think a like huh," Derrick laughed as he unzipped his pants.

"Maybe somewhat," I said, assisting him in freeing Willy again, "Damn this dick taste just like I remember," I added before diving down on it for the second time.

"Shit... seem like you been practicing though nigga... fuck... this head feel a hell of a lot better than I remember shit... take it all

the down again yo," Derrick moaned.

"Well they say things get better with age," I laughed, *"plus I miss this dick,"* I added before allowing him to push that thick pipe to the back of my throat.

CHAPTER 6: OPPS... BUSTED!

"I see you must have been dreaming about it for the last ten years," Lisa chimed in announcing herself.

"Oh shit baby I ain't even hear you coming," Derrick cried in surprise.

"Damn me either," I chimed in, jumping back in shock.

"It's cool, you just better be glad it was me and not DJ, but yall go ahead and do whatever. I got him up in the bathroom washing up for dinner and Malaysia is in the kitchen waiting to be feed, but dinner will be ready in about twenty minutes so I'll see yall

then," she stated calmly, "Oh and your welcome Shawn," she added and then turned to leave.

"Lisa wait," Derrick called after her.

"What," she replied dryly.

"Hold up y'all I ain't mean to cause no trouble, I'll just go ahead and leave after dinner," I interjected before he could say anything.

"It ain't no trouble at all baby, I already knew something was gon go down between yall. Shit for the last couple of days, every time I called your name Derrick's dick would twitch. So you just relax, go back to what you were doing, and forget about leaving. I'm surprised you waited this long to get your mouth on my man's dick, or did you suck him up while yall was on the way here too," Lisa stated, turning back to face us with a smirk on her face.

"Ummm... he actually did for a little while but I stopped him so we could actually get home," Derrick admitted shamefully

hanging his head like a child sitting in the principal's office.

"See a woman's intuition is never wrong, I'll see yall upstairs," she laughed as she started to walk off.

"Mom... Malaysia is crying," DJ yelled from upstairs.

"Ok son I'm coming," she yelled back, adding a little pep to her step.

"Dude either she is really pissed or she really doesn't care," I said.

"I know bruh them silent angers be the worst ones son," Derrick replied.

"I hope she don't turn medusa on our asses later tonight," I laughed.

"You laughing, but her ass is crazy for real. That lil Dominican woman got a temper that'll scare the hulk, but ummm... you want to go head and finish cause if she really is mad I definitely ain't gon get no pussy tonight," he said in a lustful but coy tone.

"You sure you want to do that bruh, I mean I don't want Lisa to be mad at you bruh and she had a point. What if it had been DJ that walked up on us? That would have been kind of fucked up for him to see his Padrino sucking his daddy's dick," I replied, knowing how much I wanted that dick but feeling a little hesitant to continue.

"You right, but shit... yea you right, maybe I'll just wait till Sunday when I bring you to your house," he stated.

"I don't know if I want to wait that long but if that's how it has to be I guess so," I said, "Shit I've waited over ten years so I guess two more days won't hurt," I laughed.

"You definitely right about that bruh, it's just kind of hard now since you're here and we kind of got started already," Derrick said with a bit of disappointment.

"I probably wouldn't be opposed to you returning the favor though," I stated, turning over on my belly.

"Humm I don't mind doing that

either," he replied as smile slowly spread across his face.

"Well go head and get you a taste then nigga," I taunted, rising to my knees.

"Damn this ass done got thicker too," he exclaimed as he slowly rubbed his hands across my ass.

"That's possible, I do workout four times a week," I bragged.

"Yea I see it, go head and take those sweats off so I can get a better look," Derrick said anxiously.

"Maybe I should take off my shirt and boxers too huh," I laughed, looking back at him with a grin.

"I mean I wouldn't be mad at you but if you get naked I can't be responsible for what I might do after," he stated.

"Maybe I'll just have to take a chance and see then," I replied, slipping my shirt off and then turning over onto my back as I peeled off the rest of my clothes.

"Damn son look at you all fit and shit," Derrick cried, pressing my legs back and diving on in before I could get the pants off.

"Shit nigga," I shrieked, feeling Derrick's tongue brush against my hole.

"Ass kind of taste like pussy my nigga," he said, stopping only for a moment.

"I told you I smashed the flight attendant on the way here," I reminded him.

"That bitch's pussy must have been wet as fuck because I taste it all in your ass nigga," he laughed.

"It was my nigga and that tongue is off the chain too, but if you keep eating my ass like that though you might have to do a little more than just lick it," I moaned, grasping the onto his smooth head.

"I don't know if you ready for all that just yet, but I definitely want to get inside this shit," Derrick stated, hesitantly pulling away.

"So you just gon tease me," I snapped, before wrestling him onto his back.

"I mean I... oh shit nigga..."

"Damn this dick taste good son," I growled, cutting him cutting him, "you sure I

can't get this shit inside me right now," I added, taking his dick as deep into my throat as I can get it.

"Mumm... fuck yo... Lisa gon be calling us for dinner in a bit... I... I... I don't want to start something we can't finish," he stammered.

"Ok, ok I guess I'll just go freshen up and get ready for dinner," I concurred reluctantly.

"Wait let me taste that hole again before you go," Derrick cried.

"Nah nigga if you lick it you got to stick it," I stated as I jumped up off the bed, "Plus I think you just want to taste the leftover pussy juice in my crack," I added jokingly.

"I think I already got bout all of that," he laughed.

"Yea well, unless you ready to fill me up ain't no more tasting," I said, stepping out of my pants and boxers as I turned on the

shower.

*"Come on man stop playing with me,"
Derrick groaned, jumping up to follow me.*

*"I ain't playing, all that foreplay is
only making me hornier and we can't really
do nothing at the moment so I rather not be
teased," I said, bending down to grab a towel
off the shelf.*

*"Nigga ain't nobody playing with you I
said I want to taste that hole now bring that
shit here," he said, roughly grabbing me by
the hips and pushing his face into the crack of
my ass before smacking it with his dick.*

*"That's all you doing is playing
nigga," I snapped back, bracing myself on the
wall.*

*"I'm about to show yo ass who's
playing my nigga," Derrick growled, pressing
his hard dick against my hole.*

*"Yea nigga... show me then," I moaned
as I felt his thick dick starting to enter my
hole.*

"Damn yo shit tight son," he stated as he slowly slid deeper inside me.

"Dad mom said dinner is almost ready," DJ yelled from somewhere in the staircase.

"Shit... alright son, we'll be up in a few minutes, Padrino is taking a shower," Derrick called back, quickly pulling out and yanking his pants up.

"Guess that's it for that," I laughed stepping in the shower.

"Yea DJ saved your ass," he snapped as he exited to the bathroom, "I'll see you upstairs, don't want DJ to get curious and come down here.

"Yea ok, I'll make this quick," I called behind as the warm water began to run down my body.

CHAPTER 7: DINNER TIME

About fifteen minutes later I was sitting at the table taking in the noxious aroma of the steamed broccoli that was sitting in front of me. Even though Lisa had pretty much laid out a classic Sunday evening spread I just couldn't get pass the sulfuric smell invading my nostrils. Ironically enough, broccoli was one of my favorite vegetables, however not everybody cooked it right and thus you have the odor. Needless to say I was glad when the bowl was removed from in front of me and replaced by the huge dish of chicken and rice or arroz con pollo as she called it. I guess the faces I was making gave away the displeasure

I was experiencing so Derrick decided to help me out a little. To go with the arroz con pollo and broccoli she had also prepared a summer salad with olives, grape tomatoes, and feta cheese, some roasted potatoes, cheesy jalapeno cornbread, and pineapple empanadas for dessert. She'd also concocted a virgin version of a sangria which was actually pretty good given the fact was no alcohol in it.

"So you decided to show out a bit tonight huh baby," Derrick stated while fixing a massive plate.

"Yea Lisa you didn't have to go through all this for me," I chimed in, cautiously taking my first bite.

"I didn't do for you honey I was just in the mood for all this so I cooked it, plus whatever yall don't eat you'll have for tomorrow because Malaysia and I will be out most of the day and I ain't cooking," Lisa said.

"What's going on tomorrow babe," Derrick inquired.

"Aunt Jackie is giving a surprise baby shower for Misha and you know she'll be like a chicken with her head cut off if I wasn't there to hold her hand," she replied.

"Oh yea I forgot about that, you think anybody has said anything to Misha," he asked while steadily stuffing his face.

"Knowing Aunt Jackie she might have spilled the beans herself but I'm sure my little sister will still play along," Lisa laughed.

"You're not talking about little mouth are you?" I asked.

"She's not so little now bro," Derrick stated.

"No she's not, my baby sister has grown up, gotten married, and just about finished college," Lisa added.

"Wow, wasn't she like eleven or twelve when I left," I inquired.

"Yea and now she's twenty-two, been married for a little over a year and now she's about to have her first baby," Lisa answered.

"Mom can I have some more juice now," DJ asked, innocently raising his cup in Lisa's direction.

"If you finish your vegetables I'll give you another glass," she replied.

"I did finish them mom, see," DJ said, holding his plate up to show that he'd eaten everything he was given.

"Good job son, now you might grow up to be big and strong like Padrino and me," Derrick said.

"I'm impressed too little man, I'm definitely gonna have to take you for that pizza and ice cream," I interjected.

"Yea can we go tonight Padrino," DJ cheered anxiously.

"Not tonight son, but maybe me, you, and Padrino can go tomorrow while your mom and sister are at the shower," Derrick stated.

"Ok, but can I have my juice now or do I have to eat more vegetables first," DJ asked.

"Not unless you want more vegetables," Lisa said with a straight face.

"No thank you!" DJ shrieked.

"Ok, ok, you can have the juice," Lisa laughed.

"That wasn't funny mom," he stated, staring harshly at her.

"This was pretty good Lisa," I said, scooping the last of my food into my mouth, "I didn't know you could cook like this," I continued.

"Well what kind of woman would I be if I couldn't feed my family," she replied, glaring at me coldly.

"Oh I know a couple ladies back in D.C. that can't boil water but they keep their husbands very happy," I laughed.

"Well my mother taught me very well sir and... DJ how bout you finish that juice and go get ready for bed. I'll be up in a few to tuck you in," Lisa stated, pausing in her

thoughts as she realized that her children were still sitting at the table.

"Ok mom, goodnight Dad, goodnight Padrino," DJ said, respectfully excusing himself from the table.

"Goodnight son, remember we have a big day with Padrino tomorrow," Derrick replied.

"Yea I may have a surprise for you," I added.

"Oww, I'm going to sleep right now," DJ exclaimed.

"Slow down little one, you know what we've said about running in the house," Lisa admonished.

"Careful Shawn you don't want to get on her bad side," Derrick warned when he thought Lisa was out of site.

"Man I ain't worried about no Lisa," I said boastfully loud.

"You ought to be nigga," she yelled from the stairs.

"See what I mean, she hears and sees everything," Derrick stated, sounding like a scared inmate hiding from the warden.

"Yea ok, well dinner was real good, I never had chicken and rice like that and that cornbread and those little turnover things... man... I kind of want more but I don't want to be greedy," I replied, changing subjects.

"Yea man my baby girl throws down when she feels like it, but you ain't got to be shy here bruh we all family and we know how you eat so if you want more there it is in front of you," he said.

"Nah I'm good for now but if you hear something creeping down here in the middle of the night don't shoot because it's just me," I laughed.

"I'll try to remember that," Derrick laughed.

"So Shawn, it's been ten years since you've seen this old place are you happy to be back," Lisa inquired as she entered the room.

"You know I can't quite say how I feel yet, I'm happy to see you guys but I'm sure once Tyra and my Aunt Penny figure out I'm here there's gonna be some bullshit," I replied.

"If you ask me I thought that girl was bad news from the day you met her. Then to find out that she was cheating on you with high school boys. I mean how low can a bitch be," Lisa stated.

"That's only the tip of the iceberg though, even though she was doing all the dirt she exposed Shawn and then she started spreading rumors on the man," Derrick chimed in.

"You know guys all of that wasn't so bad but the fact that my Aunt Penny was in on it and worse than that it caused problems between me and my parents. The last conversation we had was an argument over this bullshit that Tyra and Aunt Penny started.

That's what really hurt me and they're dead now so I can't go back and say anything to them," I said.

"What I don't get is why, you were wrong, you got caught, but then you turn around and try to ruin the man that's done nothing but love and support you," Derrick added expressing his disgust and confusion about the matter.

"Aunt Penny is the why," I replied, "I was getting ready to divorce Tyra but you know Penny loved her and everything that happened in our house she went cried to Penny about it. So once it was told to her that I was bi that was the icing on the cake and Penny and her pseudo spiritual clique were all on the bandwagon to ruin me," I continued.

"I don't think you're uncle being the pastor of the church helped any either," Lisa said.

"Right they saw a threat to the reputation of their church and did whatever it took to protect themselves," I exclaimed.

"Then after you left everybody was saying that you ran away," Derrick interjected.

"Exactly and before I left that was part of the argument between my dad and I, he thought I should stay and stand my ground instead stuffing skeletons in the closet and running. Not to mention the other choice words he used in reference to my lifestyle. Then my mom chimed in talking about all that money that had spent and I was still in school and hadn't really made anything of myself yet," I answered.

"But you were finishing grad school," Lisa stated puzzled by what she had just heard.

"Exactly but with the divorce, which was another sore topic, and all the other shit circulating around that little fact got swept under the rug. Then a few days later they died in a car wreck and I never got to share any of my good news with them," I explained.

"Wow, I never imagined it was all that, but like I told you earlier despite what may

have been said I know your parents were proud of you and without a doubt they loved you more than anything. I'm sure they didn't agree with everything you did, but at the end of the day you were still their son and they loved you," Derrick said, referencing the talk he'd given me in the graveyard earlier that evening.

"I agree with Derrick even though our kids are little now, I highly doubt that there's anything they could do or say that would stop us from loving them. They might get mad at us and we'll disagree but I can see me disowning either of my children," Lisa added.

"I hear yall, but truth of the matter is my parents are gone and I'll never get the chance to make things right with them. All the success I've earned means pretty much nothing because I can never come back home and say look mom or look dad this is what I did," I said, hanging my head.

"Well Shawn I can't say I know how you feel but from knowing you and knowing how your parents raised you I can say you

don't need to sit there beating yourself up about it. I know it hurts but baby at some point you've got to let go and allow your heart to heal. Forget about the bullshit and focus on what's real..."

"But what's real is what haunts me. I don't give a fuck about Tyra or Penny's old fucked up asses, I just want to be able to have peace between me and parents. They're dead yea I get that and that just makes it even harder to bear. Oh and just because I took that job and moved to D.C. doesn't mean that everything is peaches and cream. There are moments when those final words between us resound in my head like a broken record. Not to mention that dating isn't exactly easy either. When it comes to trying to explain about my divorce and all the bullshit behind it and how I ended up there in D.C. people don't really stick around," I interjected cutting Lisa off.

"Did you ever stop to think that maybe it's not the story that you're telling that people are running from but it could be that they sense the unresolved issues and guilt you

feel. I mean that's exactly what I'm saying, and we're not being insensitive to your pain but the truth is it's been ten years and your heart is still bleeding over something that you had no control over," Lisa tried to reason, placing her arms around me and cradling my head in her breast.

As she held me once again all my defense mechanisms began to fail and the tears started to fall. I hated the thought of being weak or vulnerable in front of people but I couldn't help it. The more we talked about it the more I realized just how much I was hurting and the truth of Lisa's words stung like acid. Somehow I had to find to forgive myself and let the wounds in my heart heal. Lisa and Derrick were right, my parents weren't holding a grudge against me from beyond the grave. All the bitterness and guilt I was feeling came from within and it was honestly starting to hinder me. What I needed to do was face my demons and clean out all the skeletons in my closet. I no longer hid my sexually but I wasn't out flaunting it on a flagpole either. The least I could do for my dad was be the man I was raised to be. After all being bisexual didn't mean I was some sissy parading around sucking dick and getting fucked. I was still just as masculine as I had always been and I still loved pussy for breakfast, lunch, and dinner.

CHAPTER 8: LISA'S SURPRISE

Amidst the coddling and conversation I hadn't noticed Lisa's change of wardrobe. The short spaghetti strap dress she had on when she greeted me earlier had been exchanged for silky negligée with a matching knee-length robe. I looked up to see her soft, perky breast sat prominently above the V-neck collar of her gown. Instinctively I wrapped my arm around her as she continued to hold me and lightly pass her hand over my head.

"I know this is an emotional moment and all but don't get too comfortable laying on my wife's tits bruh," Derrick stated finally rising from his seat.

"Why, you getting jealous bruh," I laughed.

"Oh nah I ain't jealous at all because I could just do this," he replied, pushing my head to the side and popping one of Lisa's tits in his mouth.

"He can do it too," Lisa retorted, pulling the top of her gown down and offering me her other breast.

"Damn ok," I said, timidly sliding my tongue around her nipple before taking the full breast into my mouth.

"Really babe, that's what's up huh," Derrick answered, seeming a little perturbed with her action.

Mumm humm, you ain't the only one that can suck on these tits. Plus I know you just did that to spite him and... damn Shawn you... shit... wait a minute baby," Lisa moaned, pulling back, obviously distracted from scolding Derrick by the feeling of my teeth sinking into her nipple.

"Sorry I got a little carried away," I apologized.

"It's ok let's go sit in the den for a minute," she suggested.

Not willing to cause any more trouble I quietly followed them into the den which sat just opposite the stairway. Once there Derrick and Lisa sat down on the sofa while I took a seat across from them on the recliner. For second I thought I saw Lisa's pussy peeking from underneath her gown but I figured I was just imagining it. Derrick was still pouting because she let me suck her tit but somehow I knew that was a front. Recalling our conversation in the guest room earlier I wondered if this was the surprise he'd mentioned. If it was the timing was sort of weird, but I'll admit having her titty in my mouth cheered me up a bit. Then just as I was getting comfortable Lisa suggested that I come sit next to them. The look in Derrick's eyes gave the notion that something wasn't going to plan but I went ahead with Lisa's request.

"Stop acting all nervous and shit, come closer to me papi," Lisa snapped, pulling me by the leg.

"He close enough bae, let the man get comfortable," Derrick interjected.

"Hush Derrick you just salty cause I let him get a taste of my tetas," she barked back as she slipped out of her robe, "Matter fact why you come over here and suck it some more," she added with a devilish grin on her face.

"Ok, ok I'll admit it I'm jealous," he cried as watched me take her breast back into my mouth.

"Mumm shit... see that wasn't hard was it," Lisa moaned, "Now you can suck mamas other one," she added.

For the next few minutes we laid there sucking Lisa's breast. Derrick seemed to calm down a little but I could tell he wasn't completely cool with it. Then just as I was getting into it again I felt Lisa's hand slide between my legs. I figured she was just caught in the moment and ignored it. Then she caught me totally off guard when she took my hand and placed it between her legs. Feeling the warm moistness of her pussy instantly made my dick hard and she took full advantage of my arousal. Squeezing and stroking my tool through my pants and moaning softly as I gently rubbed her clit. The more the moment began to intensify the more I wanted to taste her. I peeked over at Derrick to see if he was watching but he was completely engrossed in sucking the titty and getting his dick stroked. So I ceased the moment and slipped the fingers I'd been rubbing her pussy with into my mouth. She was just as sweet as I imagined she'd be and now I wanted to suck her clit even more. Knowing I needed to keep cool I restrained my desire, put the tit back in my mouth, and continued rubbing her pussy.

"Damn baby you just gon let him rub on you like that," Derrick cried, finally noticing what was happening.

"Yep and unless you want to sit back and watch him I suggest you stop whining and bring me that dick," Lisa groaned, leaning

her head back and spreading her legs open wider.

"Ok fuck it, I know you just trying to get back at me but I..."

"Yo I think I'll just stop now and go on down to bed," I announced cutting Derrick off.

"You know I think that's a good idea Shawn," Lisa agreed, "We should all go to bed," she continued, rising to her feet.

"So that's it," Derrick inquired with a confused look on his face.

"Oh no he's coming with us," she stated nonchalantly before walking off.

"Huh," I exclaimed, looking back and forth between the two of them.

"You heard my girl nigga, bring your ass on upstairs," Derrick stated sternly as he waited for me to make a move.

"Dude you was just pouting a minute ago because I was sucking her titty now you

want me to join," I replied.

"Listen man, it's either you come upstairs with us or I don't get none tonight. I know it sounds crazy but that's Lisa man," he explained.

"I'm waiting..." Lisa called from upstairs.

"Yall crazy man, but if that's what yall want I'll play along," I conceded, making my way up the stairs.

"Trust me you'll enjoy this," Derrick assured me as he followed.

Ten minutes later we were in the bedroom and I couldn't believe what was happening. Even though the three of us had been intimate before that was over ten years ago before they got married. However, here I was now eating Lisa's pussy while watching her suck Derrick's dick. Don't get me wrong I'm not complaining but I never thought this would happen again. Occasionally Derrick would smack my ass and command me to suck Lisa's clit or lick her asshole. I obediently obliged and pushed her legs back further so I could get better access to both of them. Funny thing was I really didn't need much encouragement beyond the muffled moans escaping from Lisa's stuffed jaws. After a few minutes Derrick decided it was time for him to eat the pussy so now it was my turn to get head and I didn't waste any time offering my lollipop to Lisa's mouth. While kneeling beside her I noticed an open drawer on the nightstand on the opposite side of the bed filled with lubes, oils, different sized butt plugs, vibrators, and even a whip and a pair of handcuffs. From the looks of it there was no lack of excitement in the bedroom. It even looked like Lisa might have been scratching Derrick's occasional itch for some dick. In my mind I thought about how hot it would be to see that. Derrick's thick, chocolate bubble ass was definitely some good bounty but he rarely let me inside it. However, when he did I tried to stay in that shit for as long as possible. Anyway from the looks of that drawer I knew that Derrick and Lisa's sex life was on and popping. I just hoped that a lock was kept on that so DJ couldn't get into it. Sorry I had a parental moment but now let's get back into the scene lol.

For the next few minutes I kneeled beside Lisa allowing her lips and tongue to massage my dick. I couldn't believe how good it felt, considering I was the one that taught her how to suck dick, but I loved every second of it. Remembering the days when she used to gag and bite our dicks the way she was expertly deep throating me now kind of made me proud. Slowly she milked me with her lips, cupping my balls in her free hand, swirling her tongue around the head, and making it real sloppy and nasty. Seems like my skills weren't the only ones that had improved. Then just as I was drifting off into my happy space I felt her being pulled away from me.

"No baby wait," Lisa groaned, as Derrick anxiously pulled her into missionary position, "I want to do it the way we used to do in college," she added.

"Damn bae can't I just put it in for sec," Derrick whined.

"Come on D you've had this pussy to

yourself for over ten years, don't be so selfish," I teased.

"Don't push it Shawn," he retorted.

"Come on babe I only agreed to do this so the three of us could have some fun like we used and honestly I kind of miss the way Shawn used to fuck me or watching one of yall get fucked while the other ate my pussy," Lisa stated, pulling away from him and sitting back up.

"Ugh alright, lay yo ass down nigga," Derrick snapped.

"So Lisa you was feeling my stroke game huh," I reiterated, smirking at Derrick as I laid down.

"Uh huh I was now shut up Shawn," Lisa replied as she straddled my face and nearly smothering me with her ass.

"That's what you get nigga," Derrick laughed, watching me struggle to catch some air.

"Mumm humm, just because I said I

miss the dick don't mean you the best," Lisa added before taking my dick into her mouth again.

"That's right everybody knows that daddy D is the best," Derrick said, patting his self on the back.

"I didn't say that either papi," Lisa stated, quickly popping his bubble.

"So this dick don't make you cum girl," he replied as he slowly slid into her pussy, his nuts pretty much slapping my forehead.

"Oh damn you do, you do papi," she cried, lifting up briefly while Derrick's dick its' way into her walls.

"Damn yall just gon let me die while yall argue about who the best," I exclaimed, finally catching my breath.

"You wasn't gon die nigga," Derrick laughed.

Within the next five minutes Derrick was going ham and Lisa's pussy was creaming like crazy. As I laid underneath her those sweet juices sprinkled my face like a spring shower. It wasn't every day that I got the chance to play on both sides of the fence at the same time so I was enjoying myself. I happily indulged in every moment, lapping at Lisa's clit and Derrick's balls. Occasionally I would slip my tongue into his ass which caught him off guard a little but by the way he changed his stroke I knew he loved it. All the while Lisa was clinging to my waist and sucking the skin off my dick. Then without any warning she began to squeal loudly and with each screech a gush of pussy juice sprayed on my face, into my mouth, and up my nose.

"Ahh shit... wait... what the fuck," I yelped, wiggling from under them.

"I guess you forgot she squirts," Derrick laughed.

"That wasn't no damn squirt that was a fucking waterfall and it nearly drowned my ass," I snapped, frantically wiping my face.

"I'm sorry papi, I... I just couldn't help it," Lisa moaned, falling over on one side.

"Come on bro for real are you ok," Derrick asked, still laughing.

"Nah I ain't ok, shit went all up in my damn nose," I complained.

"Aww come here papi," Lisa said, crawling over into my lap.

"My bad bro I should have warned you but I couldn't say anything because it was supposed to a surprise," Derrick empathized.

"Yea surprise nigga we gon give you a heart attack, drown you, and fuck you to death," I stated, continuing my dramatic rant.

"Aww let me kiss it and make it all better for daddy," Lisa said, taking my now limp dick into her mouth.

"The… the… the pussy when in my nose no… not my… my dick… fuck when you learn to give head like that," I managed to stammer as she skillfully brought my man back to life.

"Well you taught me some stuff and I've had a lot of time to practice," she replied.

"Shit I did a good fucking job then," I muttered.

"Let me show you what else I've learned," Lisa stated as she climbed on top of me.

"Wait, wait I think I still have some juice in my nose," I cried, feeling my dick slide into her pussy.

"Here let's put some juice in your mouth too," Derrick said, rubbing his dick against my lips.

"Fuck this pussy good man," I shouted as Lisa began showing me her skills.

"Put this dick in your mouth before you wake up the kids nigga," Derrick persisted, smearing precum all over my jaw.

"How she gripping the dick like that though," I inquired rhetorically before finally giving in and allowing Derrick's dick back into my mouth for the fourth time.

"Mumm damn nigga, don't be greedy, let my baby get some," Derrick grunted,

pulling his dick away from me and offering it back to Lisa.

"Damn really son," I moaned.

"I already know you've had plenty time with this dick honey, don't act like this yo first taste," Lisa hissed as she took him nearly balls deep while staring straight into my eyes.

"It's cool, I got this ass," I shot back, reaching up and spreading Derrick's cheeks before darting my tongue up through his crack.

"Ahh fuck, what yall doing to me," he moaned helplessly.

For the next thirty minutes or so Derrick and I took turns fucking Lisa in every position we could think of till she begged for mercy. There was so much moaning and grunting and yelling going on at one point though for sure I was gonna hear the baby crying or a knock at the door at any moment. Then the moment I had imagined became reality. When I saw Lisa reach over and pull out a strap and dildo I didn't know if I should be excited or run since she may have tried using it on me. Then Derrick laid on his back and asked me to sit on his face. As I did this Lisa began to lube him up and my eyes got as big as a small child's in a candy store. His moans vibrated through his tongue as he pressed his face into my ass. The more he licked the more I began to crave for my own hole to be filled. Still the anticipation of seeing what Lisa was going to do next had me on edge. Slowly and gently she pushed a small dildo into his ass. He clutched onto my cheeks as it penetrated his walls but took it like a champ. The dildo was no more than maybe three or four inches long but it was definitely thick enough to start opening him up for the next one. I laid there contently getting my ass ate and sucking on the head of Derrick's dick as I watched Lisa work his hole getting him ready for what she had strapped between her legs. I had only seen one guy get pegged before on a webcam and thought it was pretty hot so this was definitely a treat for me. Finally the time came and Lisa started working her makeshift dick into her husband's ass. My best friend was about to give up the cakes and I had a front row seat. However, as I watched I wanted a taste of that sweet goodness myself. Hearing him moan and feeling his tongue in my own I began to reminisce about the few times I'd been lucky enough to get it. Warm, wet, super tight, and so good it was able to make a nigga cum in minutes. I was snapped out of my daze by a Derrick biting into my cakes. Lisa had begun pumping him pretty hard and every time she went deep I would get bitten. So since I didn't want an extra hole in my ass I did the only thing that thought would make him feel better. I took his dick as deep as I could into my mouth but no sooner than when I found a good groove he flooded my mouth with cum. Letting out a loud growl of pleasure which quickly turned to begging because Lisa and I just kept going. I hadn't cum yet and I could tell Lisa wasn't ready to call it quits yet.

"Look fuck this, I've busted three times already I'm done," Derrick exclaimed, muscling his way from under us and making a dash for the bathroom.

"Somebody doesn't have the stamina

they used to huh," I joked.

"I been thinking it was just me," Lisa laughed, "But you know Derrick has always been like that, once he nuts that's a wrap," she continued.

"Well maybe you do play a part in it but shit I remember when sex was a competition for us," I stated.

"Nah that was always you Mr. Energizer Negro, busting ten nuts in a row and still stroking," Derrick said, emerging from the bathroom.

"What can I say I love sex and when it's good you don't want to stop," I replied, standing to my feet.

"Well even though you did give this pussy a good workout I don't recall you spilling any babies yet," Lisa interjected.

"You're right I didn't cum yet, but shit none of us are in our twenties anymore and I actually busted two nuts during my flight here so I'm good ma. Plus if I'm going to take my

godson out tomorrow I better get my ass to bed so I can be fresh. I've only been here a few hours and I can already see that he is a ball of energy," I said.

"What you mean you nutted during your flight," she asked, looking at me strangely.

"I did, the flight attendant invited me into the bathroom and we fucked till the FBI brought us down. Then she caught me again in my seat, sucked me up and then rode me till I nutted again," I explained calmly.

"Nigga you lying right," Lisa shrieked in disbelief.

"Nah I still got the lil note she slipped me in my bag," I replied.

"You just stick yo dick anywhere huh and you probably don't even know this girl's name," she scorned, rolling her eyes at me as she got up off the bed.

"No I don't and her name was Tina," I stated.

"Shawn I don't know what to say about you other than I ought to shove this dildo up your ass but you might like that so I'm done," she said.

"Watching how you fucked my boy I might have to take you up on that before I leave, but right now I need to get my ass to sleep," I said, pulling on my sweats, *"Oh here's that lil napkin right here, I thought I put in my carry on,"* I added, noticing the balled up piece of paper in my pocket.

"Let me see that," Derrick barked anxiously snatching it from my hand while Lisa peered around his arm.

"Meet me in the bathroom once they light goes off," they read in unison.

"See, I wasn't bullshiting," I cheered boastfully.

"I guess you have had an eventful day and night huh," Lisa said, taking the napkin from Derrick and handing it back to me.

"Why you keeping that though bruh,"

Derrick inquired.

"This is my ticket that certifies my membership into the mile high club," I laughed as I stuffed it back into my pocket.

"You are crazy, but I hope you enjoyed the surprise," he stated.

"Oh I definitely enjoyed that, even though in the beginning I couldn't tell if I should have been enjoying it or ducking for cover," I joked.

"Well Lisa is kind of unpredictable..."

"And Derrick is very selfish as you saw," Lisa chimed cutting him off.

"Well yall are married so he has a right to be a little possessive of the pussy, especially when you say shit like I missed that dick," I countered in his defense.

"Yea, yea well since the party is over I'm going take a shower, but if either of you wants to join me I'll be ready," she said, gathering the used toys off the bed and starting to walk off.

"I'll take a raincheck but I'm sure Derrick will be right behind you," I laughed.

"You damn right," Derrick cried.

"Well goodnight, Lisa I'm sure you'll be gone by the time I get up in the morning so let me get one more kiss for the road and Derrick I'll see you in a few hours," I replied, before giving her a peck on the cheek and finally making my way out of room.

CHAPTER 9: CATCHING UP

The next morning I woke up to the smell of bacon cooking. Mesmerized by the aroma I hoped up and made my way to the kitchen to find Derrick standing at the stove in his boxers. The sight of his muscular frame made my mouth water and dick twitch in my shorts. I looked around for any sign of Lisa or the kids.

"Lisa and Malaysia are gone and DJ is still sleeping," Derrick said, answering my question before I could even complete the thought.

"Well ok Daddy, I see parents really do have a sixth sense huh," I teased, stepping up

behind him.

"And a seventh and eighth one too, but yo why don't you go get DJ up while I finish making breakfast," he replied, wrapping one of his massive arms around mine.

"Ok I can do that," I answered.

"Oh and Shawn make sure you handle that bulge in your pants and don't let DJ sweet talk his Padrino into getting more sleep, it's already 10:30 and we have a pretty big day planned," he admonished, still not even looking at me.

"Ok, ok I got it, I'm sure it'll be soft by the time I get to his room," I conceded, deciding not to battle with his daddy powers. Besides he was right, I definitely didn't want to explain the reason why my dick was hard to my godson.

When I got up to the top of the stairs thoughts about last night began to meander through my head. One minute we're all sitting at the table talking about my ex-wife and my parents and I get all emotional then next thing you know we're fucking. Well played ploy though, and let's not forget how they almost drowned me. Then Lisa started sucking my dick like nothing happened, but shit I needed to think about something else because I was almost to DJ's door and reminiscing was just making my dick harder. So I tried to think about things at work, but then I remembered the temp I had smashed in my office last week. That didn't help at all so I attempted to just clear my mind and focus on the moment. When I got to DJ's room I just stood there in the doorway for a sec watching him sleep. This was probably one of the few times when he was quiet. On the other hand I guess this was a glimpse into what fatherhood was like. After Tyra had her miscarriage, something else that was swept under the rug, she had herself cleaned out. Anyway enough thinking about the past, I needed to get in this room and wake this child up before Derrick came looking for the both of us.

"Hey lil guy it's time to get up," I said, gently rocking him as I sat down on the bed.

"Aww do I have to go to school today,"

DJ mumbled.

"Well yea but today is Saturday so there's no school but your daddy is downstairs cooking breakfast for us," I stated, scooping him up under my arm.

"Oh hey Padrino, do I really have to get up now," he replied, snuggling up next to me.

"Well if you want to go get that pizza and ice cream I promised you, you got to get up," I answered, pulling him closer to me.

"I know but just a few more minutes won't hurt right," DJ asked, innocently looking up at me.

"Humm, well I don't think it would but then who wants cold grits and eggs for breakfast," I laughed.

"I don't mind them being cold, I can put it in the microwave and warm it back up," he said confidently, making himself comfortable.

"That's true but I don't daddy would

be happy if we missed breakfast," I continued to laugh.

"Ok, ok I'm up," he agreed reluctantly.

"Now go brush your teeth and wash your face, breakfast is ready," Derrick interjected from the doorway.

"Ok, ok," DJ repeated as he hopped out of bed.

"I thought you might have needed some help," Derrick said with a smile.

"And just how long have you been standing there," I asked.

"Long enough to see that Deshawn just might be capable of being a good daddy one day," he laughed.

"Oh really and just what gave you that impression," I countered, once again taking in the site of his gorgeously sculpted body.

"It's something you just know man, no puns or jokes, but I can see it in you," he replied, "Now let's go before we all have to

microwave our breakfast," he added with a smile.

About an hour later we'd finished breakfast and we getting ready to head out for our "boys day." Derrick suggested that we go see some movie that DJ had been begging to see then we'd go to the park before lunch. It seemed like a good idea to me but I wasn't so sure about seeing a kid movie. I guess that's just part of having kids right? As we made our way out the door I was a little hesitant to face the old hood but there was no turning back now. I'd made a promise to my godson so I wasn't going to back out and I was probably worrying for nothing anything. A few minutes later we were pulling into the parking lot of the movie theater and it was surprisingly empty. So went and brought our tickets, got a couple snacks, took our seats, and a couple hours later "everything is awesome" was stuck in my head. It didn't help that DJ was singing it every five minutes either but hey it's kind of catchy.

"Padrino did you like the movie," DJ asked.

"Uh yea it was cool man, what did you think about it," I replied, hoping he wouldn't ask me anymore questions about the movie.

"It was awesome!" he sang.

"So son, how bout we take Padrino to see the ducks by the lake in the park before we get lunch," Derrick suggested, changing the subject.

"Oww can we feed them too," DJ asked excitedly.

"Yea you think they would like Padrino's muscles," he asked, smiling at me.

"No they can't eat Padrino," DJ replied, sort of annoyed by his dad's dry humor.

"Why not, he's a big healthy man, I'm sure they'd love him," Derrick pressed on.

"If the ducks eat him who's going to be my Padrino?" DJ asked.

"I guess you're right son, we can't feed him to the ducks because then we'd have

nobody to buy you extra gifts and send you money and all that stuff huh," Derrick continued.

"I don't think there's anybody that can do all that like my Padrino," DJ stated confidently.

"Why is that DJ," I inquired, finally chiming in on the conversation.

"Because you're rich and you love me," DJ said plainly.

"Ok I guess that's good enough for me," I laughed.

"Who told you Padrino was rich son?" Derrick asked.

"He has a house here and a house in D.C., drives nice cars, works for the government, and he's always sending me nice things. Plus you and mom are always talking about how he makes six figures a year so I figured he's rich," DJ explained.

"Well I do have a pretty nice life these days but I'm still far from rich lil man," I

laughed, "When your mom and dad say I make six figures a year that just means I make about a hundred thousand dollars a year. I do have a condo in D.C. but the house I have here is my parents' house, do Padrino is good but he's not rich," I stated, before Derrick could tear into him.

"You get one hundred thousand dollars? Padrino do you know how many video games and candy I could buy with that? Oh and I could probably get you some real nice gifts too," he sang in awe of the seemingly large amount of money.

"Ok son, that's enough talk about Padrino's money," Derrick said sternly, as he pulled up in front of an old convenience store.

"Sorry," DJ moaned.

"Hey DJ how bout we have a little race when we get to the park," I suggested, attempting to soften the blow of Derrick's reprimand.

"Ok, and I promise I won't beat you too bad," he agreed.

"Oh really, we'll see about that," I laughed.

"This old place still looks the same huh," Derrick asked as he returned to the car.

"I was thinking it looked familiar but I wasn't quite sure where we were," I replied.

"We're not far from the house, but this used to be the spot for those hot sausage sandwiches or..."

"Those huge seafood plates for only five dollars. Is Ms. Linda still in there?" I added, remembering the place now.

"Yea she still back there cooking, but I think I saw your Aunt Penny lurking around so I just grabbed this bread and got out of there as quick as possible," Derrick answered.

"Yea I definitely don't need to see her right now," I said, rolling my eyes and shaking my head.

"Exactly, so let's move just in case it was her," he laughed.

"That ain't funny, her nosey ass would be looking all in here trying to see who you had with you," I stated.

"I know, but that's kind of what makes it even funnier. Like how can somebody really be that nosey man and on top of that she can't hold water," he laughed, as we pulled off.

CHAPTER 10: GUESS WHO

About an hour later we were being seated in Papa's Joint. I told Derrick I wanted to make another stop after we left but he advised me that we probably shouldn't risk anymore exposure. So we ordered some drinks and two split topping pizzas to sort of suit everybody's taste. DJ and Derrick wanted pepperoni, Derrick wanted supreme to his self, and I wanted the spicy Hawaiian style. Plus I also had to try their sirracha burger pizza so instead of getting four pizzas we just got two with half of each topping on them. Besides the little nibbles DJ took I basically had a whole pizza to myself and I wasn't ashamed to down it. Just meant I'd have to hit the gym extra hard when I got back home.

While we waited for the food we talked a bit about DJ was doing in school and Derrick's job and of course my life back in the nation's capital. Since we talked pretty regularly there wasn't too much that I didn't know but it was good to be able to sit and actually talk face to face. After my move most of our communication had been through, text, email, and video and phone calls. So it goes without saying that I missed the physical interaction with Derrick, not to mention seeing my godson and the intelligent individual he was becoming was a real treat.

"So I have a pitcher of root beer, one split pepperoni and supreme pizza, and one split sirracha burger and spicy Hawaiian pizza," the waitress announced as she approached the table.

"You can put all that hot stuff over there by him," Derrick stated, pointing at me.

"Eating all Lisa's cooking you should be used to spicy stuff," I replied.

"Spicy food and shit that's just hot for no reason are two different things bruh," he shot back.

"Oow daddy..."

"Hush and you better not repeat it understand," Derrick chided.

"You said it daddy," I cut in, in DJ's defense.

"Mind your manners Padrino," he snarled.

"Not intimidated papi," I countered firmly standing my ground.

"Didn't expect you would be, but we'll talk later," he stated glaring at me as if I should feel threatened.

"We shall," I replied.

"Daddy, I have to pee," DJ interrupted.

"You stay here, I'll take him. Come on DJ," I stated, snatching him up before Derrick had a chance to object.

"Padrino are we in trouble," DJ asked once we were out of Derrick's sight.

"No lil guy, your daddy can be a little abrasive sometimes and I never really liked that," I replied.

"What does abrasive mean," he asked.

"Let's just say that your daddy means well but sometimes his actions may seem a little harsh but it's to protect those he loves. Now let's get you in that bathroom before we have to explain to him why you had an accident," I explained, smiling warmly as I gently nudged him toward the door.

"Oh I didn't really have to pee, I just didn't want you guys to fight," he said as he entered the bathroom.

"Smart kid," I laughed aloud.

"He's cute too, yours?" a familiar voice asked.

"He's my godson actually but umm…" I answered, almost choking on my words when I realized it was Tina.

"Don't be so happy to see me," she laughed with a smile.

"I'm not... I mean... I thought you'd be working... what are you doing here in Violet?" I stammered.

"Calm down love it's ok, I kind of have that effect on people, but I called in sick so I could go to a baby shower with my cousin. So I'm guessing this must be home for you," she asked smiling seductively.

"Yea unfortunately it is, but I haven't been here in a while so here I am," I answered.

"Say no more honey when I got the chance to leave home I was all over it," she continued to laugh.

"Padrino I'm finished," DJ announced as he took hold of my waist.

"Did you wash your hands," I asked.

"Yes sir," he answered respectfully.

"Well hello handsome, how are you,"

Tina inquired, bending her knees slightly to get closer to DJ.

"I'm ok," he answered hesitantly after looking up at me and clinching tighter to my shirt.

"I'm sorry he's a little shy around strangers," I apologized.

"No worries, but it was good to see you again Shawn, maybe we can hang out a bit before I leave, but I got to get out of here now if I'm going to be on time for this shower," she said as she turned to leave.

"Ok that would be nice, good seeing to you too," I replied, watching her ass giggle as she walked away.

"Who was that lady Padrino," DJ asked.

"She worked on the airplane that brought me here, but what was that shy act about," I answered with a question of my own.

"She was pretty and had big tetas," he

replied as we approached the table.

"Big tetas... ummm I thought you were taking him to the bathroom," Derrick stated, picking up on our conversation.

"I did, but while he was using the bathroom I ran into an old friend," I laughed.

"She was sexy daddy," DJ chimed with big grin on his face.

"DJ," I laughed, listening to my godchild talking about a woman as if he was grown.

"What? She was and those tetas were almost bigger than mommy's," he added before innocently going back to eating his pizza.

"And you wonder why I'm so hard on him," Derrick stated, staring at DJ in disbelief.

"Oh no I get it, but let him look at the tetas and think women are sexy. At least we know that he's wired right," I laughed.

"I'm glad you're amused by it, but don't look now but when I tell you to turn around slowly," he said looking over my shoulder.

"You really gon tell me to not look, that just makes me want to look even more," I said.

"Ok, ok look now," he said.

"That's not who I think it is right," I said after taking a quick glance back at the counter.

"Yea it's definitely her bruh," Derrick confirmed.

"Oh boy..."

"I already know, you want to jet before she recognizes us and comes over here," Derrick interjected, basically reading my mind.

"I think that might be best," I agreed, signaling for the nearest employee.

"How can I help you," a young white

guy said.

"Can I get the check and box for his pizza," I stated.

"Sure I'll be right back," he replied, quickly dashing off.

In no less than maybe ten minutes later we'd cashed out and were in the car. Hopefully my ex-wife hadn't seen us and my cover was still intact. It was enough that I'd have to deal with them at church tomorrow and God knows what kind of foolishness would be stirred up.

"So Shawn who was this friend you met that has my son's hormones jumping," Derrick inquired.

"It was Tina," I replied.

"The flight attendant?" he asked.

"Yea, I was surprised too and DJ was acting all shy with her but he obviously liked what he saw," I joked.

"Obviously, but yo I got to get some

gas or else we'll be walking home. You gonna be ok," Derrick stated as we turned into a shell station.

"Yea as long as there's no more surprises I'm good," I laughed.

"Well this shouldn't take too long," Derrick said, closing the door behind him.

CHAPTER 11: CAT'S OUT THE BAG

As I sat there in the car I began to think about all that had happened in the last forty-eight hours. I was dreading this trip and I'm still a little apprehensive about seeing certain people, but on the other hand it's been pretty interesting. Tomorrow I was definitely going to have to deal with whatever came my way and there was no turning back. I came here for some long overdue time with my friends and godchild, but there was also some matters I needed to tend to with my parents estate. There weren't any bills or legal issues, but the house was just sitting there empty. With the exception of my dad's BMW, I'd sold or given the vehicles away to other family members. I

*decided I was going to take it back to D.C.
with me and over the next couple days I would
be deciding if I was going to sell the house or
rent it out.*

*"Hey, I thought that was you I saw at
the store earlier," a high-pitched female rang
along with a tap on the glass.*

*"Hi," I replied dryly, realizing it was
my Aunt Penny.*

*"So you move away and now you're
too good to give your aunt a proper greeting?
Boy get out of this car and give me a hug,"
she snapped.*

*"Forgive me, how have you been Aunt
Penny," I said, attempting to muster up every
ounce of charm I could as I stepped out of the
car and gave her a big hug.*

*"Now that's better, I haven't seen you
in what ten years? You sure have grown to be
a nice looking man. I mean you do still call
yourself a man don't you," she stated, looking
me over with a scrutinizing eye.*

"Excuse me," I asked, not completely sure I'd heard her right.

"I mean you did have that little problem sleeping with other men, so I didn't know if you played the man or the woman," she continued without an inkling of concern or respect for me.

"Well I still have a dick so I guess that makes me a man don't it," I retorted frustrated with her lack of tact. Not to mention DJ was sitting in the backseat and I'm sure the commotion had woke him up.

"How dare you talk to me like that," she barked, smacking me on the cheek, "I've never been so disrespected in my life," she added, lifting her hand to strike me again.

"Maybe you should have thought about that before you opened your mouth and disrespected me," I shouted back, catching her hand this time.

"Listen boy I don't know who you think you talking to but you ain't too old for me to bust your tail out here," she threatened taking

a step back.

"I'd like to see you try it you old..."

"Hey that line was kind of long in there I'm a just get gas in the morning," Derrick announced as returned to the car just in time.

"Oh hi Derrick, I didn't realize your son was back there since my nephew seems to have lost his manners," she chirped, changing her tone when she noticed DJ staring at her.

"Yea well we've got to get home so we can start dinner for Lisa," Derrick replied as he got in the car.

"Oh well don't let me hold you baby and I hope I'll see you all at church tomorrow," she stated, backing away from the car.

"Of course," Derrick stated.

"See you later nephew," she smiled, before walking away.

"Let's get out of here," I barked, still a little angry from my encounter.

"DJ are you ok buddy," Derrick asked, taking a look into the backseat before pulling off.

"Yes but why was the church lady picking on Padrino?" he questioned.

"Some people just don't know how to be nice," I answered.

"But what did she mean when she said you had a problem with sleeping with men," DJ continued to inquire.

"She said that to you in front of him," Derrick asked.

"Along with some other bull that I won't repeat, but now you see why I was ready to cut into her," I replied.

"Well I'm glad I came out when I did because it looked like it was about to get ugly and I can't believe she would say that in front of my son," Derrick said, getting more and frustrated.

"But what did it mean," DJ reiterated, "She said some real nasty things to Padrino,"

he added.

"Well when I was younger I was married but it didn't work out and during our divorce there was a lot of name calling and rumors being spread, and that was one of them," I explained.

"But what does that mean?" DJ asked again.

"She was saying that your Padrino was gay son," Derrick chimed in.

"But Padrino isn't gay is he? That lady at the restaurant looked like somebody he had smashed and she wanted more," DJ said plainly.

"Son where did you learn that and how would you know what it looks like," Derrick questioned, taken back by DJ's comment.

"Kids at school talk about it all the time," he stated innocently.

"Well your Padrino is not gay and yes I did smash her, but let's keep all that kind of talk between us guys. I don't know how your

mom would feel about you saying stuff like that," I said.

"Lisa would flip," Derrick laughed nervously.

"Padrino I don't think you should talk to her anymore, she's a bully," DJ suggested.

"Well unfortunately she's my aunt so I don't really have much of a choice while I'm here," I laughed.

"Aww man, well as long as she doesn't hit you again we'll be ok," DJ stated.

"Well I'm glad to know you have my back lil guy," I laughed, "Hey D there's another gas station you want to try getting gas again," I continued.

"I don't know bruh, I think I'm a just wait till later. We don't need you to cause anymore scenes," Derrick joked.

"Me! She attacked me bruh," I cried.

"I know, I know I was just messing with you," he laughed.

CHAPTER 12: BACK TO THE SCENE

After the run in with my aunt we decided to go on back to the house, after Derrick stopped and filled up the car at another station. I couldn't believe that after ten years the first thing she would bring up is my sexuality. However, I didn't really expect much good from any of my family and she confirmed. Let's also not forget that she said all shit in front of DJ and I know Derrick was pissed about it. Especially since he started questions about the things she said. I did think it was a little funny though that DJ was already talking about sex and liking women and Derrick was pretty lost for words. Anyway, once we got back to the house

Derrick pulled out the leftovers for us and DJ wanted to finish his pizza. Then after we ate we watched a couple movies on Netflix while we waited for Lisa and Malaysia to get home.

The next morning it was time for me to move on to my next destination. I hadn't really spent much time there since my parents died but for the next couple days it's where I'd be staying. By this point I knew the whole neighborhood knew I was there, thanks to Aunt Penny. So I gathered my things and prepared myself to walk back through those doors for the first in ten years. Derrick and Lisa tried to persuade me to stay there and just go to the house when I needed to, but I felt it may do me some good to stay in the house. I also figured if there was to be anymore confrontations it would better not to be around the kids.

"Hey Shawn if you want something to eat before you go Lisa cooked some grits, ham, eggs, and toast," Derrick announced as he peeked into the door.

"Ok, but what you peeking for nigga,"

I laughed.

"I wasn't peeking I was being courteous, now bring your ass upstairs and get some food," he replied before walking off.

"Hey if you like what you see it's ok bro," I called behind him.

"Whatever dude," he yelled back.

When I got upstairs everybody was sitting at the table. The smell of the eggs and ham seemed to draw me in and once again Lisa had the table laid out. Aside from the main items Derrick told me about there was an array of jams, syrup, and butter. If I lived nearby I could really get used to this.

"So Shawn are you sure you don't want to stay here the next few days? We have plenty room and I'm sure the kids would love to have you around," Lisa said before I could get even get to the table.

"Well good morning, and I wouldn't mind but I really need to get in there and sort through some stuff plus I've arranged some

appointments with a couple agents since I'm considering selling it. Not to mention a little time in the house might actually help me to really deal with them being gone. I think the discussion we had Friday night made it obvious that I never really dealt with it," I replied.

"How much paperwork could there be? Given the house has been sitting up a while and it might need some cleaning and maybe some minor repairs, but... I'm just saying we're here and our doors are open man," Derrick commented as he began to stuff his face.

"Exactly you're not alone Shawn and despite what may happen today we've got your back," Lisa stated.

"Yea we got your back Padrino, especially if that church lady messes with you again," DJ interjected.

"Church lady? What is he talking about?" Lisa asked.

"We ran into Penny on the way home

yesterday and it didn't go so well," Derrick replied.

"Oh wow, what happened?" she inquired.

"We exchanged some words, she smacked me, and Derrick came out the store right when she was threatening to beat my butt. The worse part thought is that DJ heard a lot of what was said and... well... things had to be explained," I answered.

"Son is this true?" Lisa questioned, turning her attention to DJ.

"Yes maim, but Padrino promised to stay away from the church lady bully, but mommy why do people spread rumors about other people," DJ asked.

"I don't really know baby, but some people are just mean, cruel, and have nothing better to do with their time but try and make other people miserable," she answered.

"Sometimes people don't know how to deal with the truth so they make up their own

truths which might not always benefit everybody," I added.

"But that doesn't make since Padrino," DJ stated, looking at me curiously.

"I know lil guy, and that's why it doesn't pay to spread rumors about people. The real truth will eventually come out and you might not like the consequences that come with it," I said.

"Well said Shawn, and I guess that means you've really got a reason to go to that house," she affirmed.

"That's what I've been saying every time yall bring it up," I laughed.

"Yea ok well when you're ready I'll take you on over there," Derrick stated as he finished his plate.

"I see why you work out so much now, you eat like a horse and I thought I was greedy," I joked.

"Yea whatever, I don't eat any more now than I did ten years ago" he said while

reaching for another piece of ham and a scoop of eggs.

Thirty minutes later Derrick and I were on our way to my parents' house. Since church was at noon, I had roughly two hours to get settled a bit and make my way there. DJ had persisted on tagging along but Derrick made him stay put so he could bathe and get ready for Sunday school. It sort of broke my heart to see his sad little face peeking out of the window as we pulled off but it was for the best. The drive from Derrick and Lisa's to my parents was only about five or ten minutes yet it seemed like an hour. Maybe I was just starting to have cold feet again however I couldn't turn back. I knew if I said the word Derrick would turn around but that was too easy. I had to go and face the ghosts of my past starting with the feelings of guilt and sorrow I still felt for my parents. I needed time to kick, scream, shout, and be angry and let all my emotions out. Something I just couldn't do with other people around.

When we finally pulled up to the house it was like time just stopped. Memories and images of my last moments with my parents, which had been a constant nightmare for the last ten years, flooded my mind. I needed to get out of the car but something was holding me back. Though I knew I still had all functionality, for those moments it was like I was paralyzed. I could feel Derrick's hand on my shoulder and faintly here him saying something but I was frozen in time and space. Being forced to replay every moment of that night and then call a couple days later that they were gone.

"Shawn, Shawn, Shawn can you hear me," Derrick cried, shaking me back to reality.

"I'm good, I'm good, I just blanked out for a second," I said, grabbing his hand.

"Are you sure you want to do this Shawn? We can go back to the house, call some people in the morning, and let them handle it," he suggested.

"Nah I didn't come all the way here to take the easy way out. I need to settle the issues that I left unresolved so I can finally

have peace with the decisions I've made," I replied.

"Ok well if you want me to I'll walk in with you," he said.

"Thanks," I replied.

Once I gathered the strength to get out of the car I noticed that somebody had been keeping the lawn. When I questioned Derrick about it he informed me that he had been doing it at least once a month. He also told me that he occasionally came and checked around inside and started the car to make sure it was still running. I was a bit curious how he got into the garage but then I remembered he had a key. When I left home I forgot to collect the spare that was always hidden somewhere around the door. So I called Derrick and told him to find it and just keep it for safe keeping. However, I didn't think that he would take on the responsibility of looking after the house for me.

"So we're here," I said as I opened the door.

"Yep, we had some good times in this place," Derrick boasted.

"We did, but the only memory I can recall at the moment is that argument," I replied.

"Shawn you've got to stop beating yourself up about that. Remember the premise of the argument was those bullshit rumors that Tyra and Penny started," he stated in an attempt to keep me from another emotional trip.

"Maybe so but there was truth in those rumors, I am bisexual, and when I told my parents that along with the fact that Tyra and I were getting divorced it only added heat to the fire. They knew I'd never cheat or compromise my integrity," I countered, taking a seat on the sofa, "You know my dad was one of the best lawyers in this area and for word to get out that his son was doing ungodly things with other men was a smudge on his reputation. Let's not forget that I had been in school forever and still didn't have a good job and..."

"Shawn stop, a lot of those things that were said that night were said out of frustration and again regardless of what truth there may have been in you actually sleeping with men. The whole thing would have never happened if your ex-wife and aunt wouldn't have been going around gossiping about you. Not trying to point fingers or plant any seeds but it's the truth," Derrick said, cutting me off.

"I don't know if I can say that it's totally their fault but I do get where you're coming from. However, if you look at it that way maybe I should have never told Tyra I was bi," I replied.

"No you did the right thing confiding in your wife and not keeping any secrets from her, but she was wrong in telling all your household business to Penny," he exclaimed, taking a seat next to me.

"D I know you're my friend and you're gonna do everything in your power to support me, but..."

"Hold on bruh, you're right about me

being you're friend and that being so I'm not going to let you keep beating yourself up over something that you had no control over. I mean I don't what all was said between you and your parents but I'll never just say shit to make you feel good. The truth is the truth and you need to open your eyes and see it instead of imprisoning yourself in guilt," he interjected again.

"Ok, ok I hear you, I just need to process all this and even though what you said makes sense it doesn't change the fact that my last interaction with my parents was a fight. That's something I can't ever change," I said, looking up at the picture of the three of us sitting on the mantle.

"As true as that may be, we both know that your parents loved you and despite the harsh words here and there they were proud of all the things that you had accomplished. Now I'm a go and get myself ready for church, if you need me call me," Derrick stated as he stood to his feet.

"Aight, I'll see you there," I said.

"You shouldn't have any problems with the car, I started her up last week and she runs like a charm. You might to change the tires and do a little routine maintenance on it when you get the chance though," he said with a smile.

"Ok I'll keep that in mind," I replied nonchalantly.

"Hey man come here," Derrick

said as he pulled me up into his arms, "I know it's hard, but you're going to get through this. Keep your head up aight," he continued, embracing me tightly.

"I know, I just got to fight my way through," I replied, taking shelter in the comfort of his arms for the second time.

"Well I'm here for you my dude, but right now I really do need to get home so I can get ready because Lisa will kill me if we're late for church," he laughed.

"Aight man I'll see you guys at the church. I need to start getting myself together

as well, maybe we can all go out to eat tonight, my treat," I suggested.

"Ok I'll run it pass Lisa and let you know," Derrick said, heading toward the door.

"Ok you do that," I laughed.

CHAPTER 13: NO MORE RUNNING

For about twenty minutes or so after Derrick left I just sat there in the living room looking around at old pictures. Just like Derrick had said there were a lot of good memories in this place. As I stared at the pictures I began to recall the stories behind them. I could almost feel the joy and pride that was felt in those moments. The smiles on my parents' faces brought me a little comfort, but deep down I was still in pain. Yet time was ticking and I needed to get up and start getting ready. So I .28/9+*9forced myself up off the sofa, grabbed my bags, and headed upstairs. As I made my way through the house I began to feel sort of uneasy. It was almost as *if someone was watching me or following me, but I knew I was alone. When I got to the top of the stairs I looked around, debating if I should go to my old room or dare the taboo of entering my parent's room. Noting that time was ticking I decided to just take residence in one of the guest rooms for now. For a family of three this was a pretty big house, five bedrooms, three and half bathrooms, large living and dining areas, huge gourmet kitchen, and an office just to name a few of its attributes. At times I wondered what made my dad buy such a big house.*

Ten minutes later I'd pulled myself together and after a few more tears I rinsed it all away with the warm waters of the shower. I thought extensively about what Derrick said and I knew he was right. All these years I'd held myself captive to a memory that nobody but God had the power to change. Let's also not forget about the rumors that had been spread and me conveniently getting a job out of state just as everything was hitting the fan. Now after all these years here I am getting ready to face all my demons at once. This was either going to be a big mistake or a step in the right direction. I laid back again the wall of the shower and closed my eyes. As the warm water ran down my body I began to say a little prayer.

"Son, we love you and we're proud of the man you've become," I heard a familiar voice say, snapping me back to reality. I looked around but there was no one there, however, that eerie feeling was back. Strangely enough though, the voice sounded like my mom, but the idea of her speaking to me from the dead was a bit crazy. Maybe I had drifted off for a second and was dreaming, and maybe the notion of someone else being there was all in my head too. Not knowing what to make of it I just proceeded to wrap up my shower and get ready for church.

Within the next thirty minutes I'd managed to get dressed and make my way over to the church. When I arrived I could hear music but there was still a good bit of people outside in the parking lot. Most of which who would stop and stare as I circled around in effort to find a spot. I was sure my

Aunt Penny had made my presence in the neighborhood known so it was expected. Finally I found an empty space but before getting out I just sat there for a minute and thought about all that could happen when I walked through those doors. The stares and fingers pointing were already making me uncomfortable. Maybe they didn't know who I was but they sure didn't make me feel welcome either. So after a mental debate I drug myself out of the car with the new bag DJ gave me strapped over my shoulder.

"Good afternoon, welcome to Shiloh," a young lady with a warm smile said as she handed a program and an offering envelope. I smiled gracefully and continued on inside. In a matter of seconds I spotted Lisa, Derrick, and DJ or maybe I should say DJ spotted me. Cheerfully announcing to his parents that Padrino was there and I had the bag. That of course attracted the attention of some other folks as well, but the excitement of my godchild put a smile on my face. Especially after the frowns and tears he displayed when I left that morning. So I took a seat next to them

and actually enjoyed choir even though the music was a bit dated.

For the next forty-five minutes I sort of felt a peace. Listening to the music, hearing the prayers being lifted, scriptures being read, and now it was time for the word. When my uncle stepped up to the mic I expected a grand production about his nephew being home. However, he did more than just acknowledge me, his entire message was about me. He started off with the story of the prodigal son then somehow he tied that into Sodom and Gomorrah and then went on this spill about homosexuals, people with no morals, and to top it off he went on about how children should honor their parents. Basically wrapping his opinions about me in a half-baked sermon targeted directly at me. I was hurt, mad, and disgusted all at the same time and I couldn't take another second of it. So I grabbed my bag and headed out towards the door.

"Hold on baby, isn't that how the pot started boiling in the first place," a female voice said from behind me.

"So what am I supposed to do just sit there and be humiliated," I replied, clinging to the door handle.

"By trying to shame you they only make a spectacle of themselves, but if you don't learn to stand your ground you're always going to look guilty. The bible says that it's the will of God that you silence the ignorance of fools by doing good. You had your rough patch with the divorce and accepting your sexuality but you're a college grad with a good job. It's not too many young black men from around here that move away and do well and I know Gina and Daniel would be proud if they could see you now," she answered, placing a hand on my shoulder and turning me to face her.

"But Ms. Angelica I don't know if I want to be bothered with all this anymore. I have a good life in D.C. and if it wasn't for the need of wanting to see my friends and godchild and some other matters I would have never come back here," I stated.

"Baby I understand, believe me I do.

Your mom and I were friends for a long time and though you may have some of Daniel's looks and build, you're smart and head strong like Gina. You have that fight in you just like she did but I feel like there's something holding you back. It's almost like you really do feel guilty about their deaths and you rather pull away than face the music, but baby listen that's not the way. I don't quote scripture just because it sounds nice or looks good in front of people, it's because I know God for myself and I've lived through enough to have a testimony. People have tried to tear you down, but look at you now. A strong, educated, black man with a successful career and I'm sure there are plenty folks waiting for you to get back so they can get a taste. But listen to me and listen to me good love, those dreams you've been having and those voices you heard aren't just your mind playing tricks on you," Angelica said, firmly taking my hand in hers.

"Wait a minute how did you know about that? I never said..."

"Honey you didn't have to say a word,

the look on your face and the Holy Spirit speaks very clearly. God has been trying to get you to let go of that for years but you so stubborn you want to hold on to it and feel guilty, feel sorry for yourself. It's time for you to stop that and I mean right now. You keep holding on to that baggage and you gon find yourself in a mental prison that nobody but the good Lord can get you out of," she interrupted.

"But I don't even know where to begin," I replied, remorsefully dipping my head down.

"You can start by drying those tears and holding your head up. Don't let your parents' memory be tarnished by foolery and drama you need to get in there and set the record straight my love," she stated.

"I don't know how to do that exactly but I guess if I need to confront some people and get some things off my chest I this is the place to do it right," I asked, in a half-hearted effort to sound bold.

"Within reason yes it is, just remember

who you are and whose you are baby. You do what you can and let the Lord do the rest. Time to stand your ground and stop running from this," Angelica said sternly.

"Yes maim," I said respectfully as I turned to return to the sanctuary.

I was a bit weirded out by some of the things she said but in my heart I knew she was right. I wasn't heavy into church like my parents but I did know God. I believe if it hadn't been for Him and the prayers that were lifted on my behalf I may not be where I am today. So if the dreams I've been having and the voices I heard this morning were supposed to be some kind of sign I had no choice but to move forward. As I made my way back to my seat I noticed that my uncle had concluded his message and another guy was up speaking. I asked Lisa who he was and she informed me that he was the district overseer for southeast Louisiana. Bishop Carl Tolbert or something like that, and as he spoke he didn't seem too pleased with my uncle but he kept his remarks tactful.

"Excuse me young man could you come up to the front for a second," he said noticing that I'd returned. I was a bit hesitant to move after the first spectacle but I had to be obedient, "I understand that you're Elder Daniel and Evangelist Gina's son," he added.

"Yes sir I am," I answered.

"Listen I'm sure this may not be easy for you but I'd like you to say a few words to the congregation. You're uncle and aunt have done a pretty good job of making you look bad but I don't see any of that in you. Yet I do notice a bit of guilt in your eyes, you care to share son," he urged as a mic was placed in my hands.

"Well... I... really wasn't expecting this, but at the same time I wasn't expecting a message targeted at ridiculing me either," I began, looking out at the congregation of whispering lips and stoic faces, "But ten years ago my world felt completely apart when I lost my parents. My dad, he was my idol and my mom was my rock. Whenever I needed advice or a prayer or just a hug she was there for me.

The sting of that lost was deepened though by the fact that we never got the opportunity to reconcile after an argument we'd had about other things that were going on in my life. Their deaths hurt even more because I never got to tell them I was finally graduating with my masters and the same day I walked the stage with no one there to support me but my friends Lisa and Derrick was the same day I laid them to rest. Many of you might remember that not long before that Sis. Tyra and I were going through a divorce. What many of you don't know is that contrary to the rumors of me sleeping around, bribing teachers for grades, and having all kinds of STD's she had been cheating on me. The one true love of my life that I'd trusted with everything took my heart and spit on it. Something else that even my close friends don't know is that my one chance at fatherhood was ripped from me by that same woman's irresponsibility and spite. However, I'm not here to point fingers or make anyone look bad, but I do want to clear the air. Back then I was going through so much I didn't have the strength to fight, but today someone reminded me how strong I am and how valuable I am. I won't stand here and debate anything or toss back jabs at the people who tried to hurt me but I will continue to do well. Since I left here I've had my regrets but my life has honestly never been better. I have a great job working for the federal government, I make a substantial amount of money, and I have a nice home. What many of you, including my deceased father, saw as me running away was only me grabbing hold of the blessing God had laid out for me. So no I won't combat anyone with vindictive words or actions, but I'll do as the word says and continue silencing ignorant fools by doing good," I stated, standing firm with my shoulders square looking out at all the scrutinizing faces.

"Well young man, I believe what you just did took a lot of courage and it may have just been the first step to your healing. People often make the mistake of learning a person through a listening jar and they miss all the truth of who that person really is. We should never be guilty of judging another firstly because the word of God plainly says, 'judge

ye not, less you be judged.' Then secondly because you never know the test that, that person has been through to gain the testimony that they hold. Son I want you to get my information after service and I want to pray with you on weekly basis. I believe God has some great things in store for you but first you've got to let go of the past. Pouring salt on open wounds will only continue to sting until you decide to step back and let them heal," he encouraged before releasing my back to my seat and proceeding to close out the service.

CHAPTER 14: SPIRITS REST

After the service I decided to make another visit to the graveyard. This time I was going alone and I was determined to get out as much frustration and emotion as I could. It was time for me to have some peace with all this and I wasn't leaving that tomb till I got what I came for. When I got in the car I just sat there for a minute thinking about what had just happened. I didn't know if it really made any difference to anybody else but I actually felt better. It was also kind of comical to see Ms. Angel's words come to life not minutes after she'd spoke them.

"Hey Shawn," Derrick cried as he

tapped on the glass.

"Yo what's good man," I replied, a little startled by the interruption.

"Dude I just wanted to say I'm proud of you. That was pretty amazing what you did in there," he said with a smile, "Oh and I talked to Lisa on the way over and she's game but thinks we should invite some people so we can all talk a bit more," he continued.

"Well I don't know how much good it did, but in a way I feel a bit better," I stated.

"That's what matters bro, but hey what you bout to get into," he asked.

"I'm a take a drive to the graveyard and then head to the house and chill till we get ready to go eat," I answered, looking him squarely in the eye.

"Hey I'm not even going to say anything if you feel that's what you need to do go for it. I just want you to be careful man and if you need..."

"No I don't want you to come, I'm

going alone and I'll see you later," I stated sternly.

"Ok, ok but one more thing," Derrick conceded.

"I'm listening sir," I replied.

"Thanks for using the bag, DJ was real happy to see that," he said.

"There's no need to thank me for that," I laughed.

"I know but the look on my son's face when he saw you was priceless. Shit I'm almost jealous because I don't always get that kind of reaction out of him," Derrick laughed, "But seriously that kind of happiness is something you can't buy man," he reiterated.

"Well I guess I'll get my chance at knowing what that's like one day," I joked.

"Yea and bout that, how come you never told me?" he inquired.

"I don't know but we'll talk about that later man. I'm a get on out of here before

anymore fingers get pointed," I stated, looking around at the people milling around.

"Ok, well call me if you need me bro," Derrick said, backing away as I started the engine.

About two hours later I was pulling into the driveway of my parents' house. My time at the graveyard was pretty good. I spent most of the time crying and praying, but I also got a chance to really talk and get my feelings out. What I didn't expect though was to see my ex-wife sitting on the steps when I got to the house. I didn't know how long she'd been sitting there but I did have a pretty good idea of how long she was going to stay.

"Shawn before you say anything, I just want to say I'm sorry for what I did but..."

"Oh wow there's a but," I interjected, folding my arms.

"Let me finish," she pleaded.

"Ok go head," I stated coolly.

"I don't think what was said needed to

be said, even though your uncle was wrong I think our business should have stayed our business..."

"Ok you can stop right there, so it was all good for people to think of me as some low life, disease infected, faggot with no moral compass, but when the truth about you comes out you there's a problem? You're crazier than I thought ma," I laughed, brushing passed her as I went up to the door.

"Shawn that's not what I meant... well... maybe but look I didn't come here to fight with you," Tyra said, scrambling to gather her thoughts.

"So what did you come here for? You miss me? You want some dick? No I'm sure you still get plenty of that. Maybe you realize what you lost now and feel guilty or something. I mean what could you possibly want from me," I snapped, turning back to face her.

"Look I'm sorry ok, I never meant to hurt you but Penny said..."

"Penny again huh, you never got the message did you? That's my aunt but that old bitch is poison to everything and everyone she touches. Seems that you were no exception to that," I interrupted again.

"Shawn I do get it, that's why I'm here. I know it was my fault that things went the way they did between us, and I should have never trusted Penny with our secrets. I just figured that since she was family as well as our pastor's wife she would be a good confidant," she stated, taking a step towards me.

"Did something happen between the two of you," I asked, noticing the vulnerability in her eyes.

"You mean other than being caught in the middle of a lethal word game and destroying my marriage? Or would you rather know what happened after you left?" she countered.

"I'm not sure if I really care but sure go ahead and tell me," I replied.

"Can we go inside and talk please? Last thing I need is more bullshit from the Holy Roller crew," Tyra requested.

"At this point I don't really want you on this property let alone inside my parents' house," I huffed.

"Shawn please," she pleaded.

"Those puppy dog eyes won't get you any empathy from me honey plum," I laughed.

"Shawn if you ever loved me please just give me a few minutes and hear me out," she continued to implore.

"Oh now you want to try and play tug of war with the heart strings. Listen... I don't know what kind of drama popped off after I left here and frankly I really don't give a fuck. I'm just here to finalize some business and close this chapter in my life for good. Now I tried telling you to stop running your mouth to her about everything that went on but you just said fuck me and did what you wanted to do. Including cheating on me while you were pregnant and killing our baby. Hell with all

the dirt she has on you I wouldn't be surprised if she doesn't turn it against you," I stated calmly but assertively.

"She did turn on me!" Tyra exclaimed, "After you left there was a slight disagreement between us and well things didn't go her way and she..."

"She told everybody what whore you were," I interjected, "You I'd love to feel sorry for you but I stopped feeling things for you a long time ago. I don't hate you or anything, but I just don't care to be bothered with your manipulative bullshit. So it was nice of you stop by but I've got plans and I need to get ready. Good luck with whatever you've got going on and God bless you," I said, turning back around to unlock the door.

"I knew it was a bad idea coming here," she mumbled.

"So why'd you come then," I snapped, "Never mind don't answer that, just get off my property," I added before closing the door and leaving her standing there on the steps.

Now I know I might have been a bit cruel but my ex-wife was an ex for a reason and I wasn't about to give her a window to crawl into. She gave her little apology, I'm good, and that's all the conversation that was needed between us. There's no need for her to come crying on my shoulder about anything which was probably all bullshit anyway. I know, I know the bible says I should have compassion even to those who hurt me. I get it, but like I told her that day I have no malice in my heart towards her, however, I was completely done with her, case closed.

Fifteen minutes later I found myself sprawled out on the sofa. After watching Tyra pace around and sulk for a few minutes before finally leaving I just laid there. Thoughts of the day's events so far meandered through my head. I wondered who these other people were that Lisa wanted to invite to dinner. Hopefully it wouldn't be any more drama because I'd had my fill of that for one day. The day hadn't been all bad though. I felt like a lot of weight had been lifted off my shoulders by just talking and taking time to pray. Let's not forget how my uncle tried to embarrass me but then ended being reprimanded. They say karma takes no prisoners and I saw that first hand today. I also thought about the words that had been spoken to me by the bishop, let go so you can move forward. I'd be remised if I said I hadn't heard those words before, quite a few times actually. Lisa, Derrick, Ms. Angel, and then a complete stranger, you think I got the message yet? Even though I feel like some good progress was made by letting things out I won't sit here and make it seem like everything is all good now because it's not. However, I think I'm finally coming to grips with the fact that the past is just that and there's nothing I can do about it except live and do my best to make the future better. I guess by this point somebody reading may be saying just get over it already and I am, but until you've experienced pain like I have you won't know how difficult it can be to just get up and brush yourself off. Healing is a process and it doesn't happen overnight, just thought I'd add that in there.

As I laid there the minutes turned to

hours and before I knew it, it was after six. I looked at my phone and saw that I had two missed calls and a couple text from Derrick. I guess it might have been reasonable to say that he was worried about me since his last text said, "I'M ON MY WAY OVER THERE." Then before I could even start to type a response there was a loud banging on the door followed by the sound of a key being wiggled into the lock. I knew he was going to have some choice words for me but I couldn't stress about it.

"Yo bro, I just woke up and saw the calls and text, I'm good I was just a bit drained after everything," I tried to explain as he walked through the door.

"Nigga do you know how fucking worried I was that something might have happened to you or... I won't say that but dude really," Derrick barked.

"Derrick I understand for real, but look when I got back here Tyra was outside waiting for me. Long story short, she gave me some half-hearted ass apology and then tried

to feed me some bullshit about her falling out with Penny and blah, blah, blah," I said.

"Oh that wasn't no bullshit, Penny dogged the piss out of her because after you left she tried to stand up for you," Derrick informed me, "But nigga I'm still mad. You got me worried about your ass and you laid up in this bitch slobbering and clutching your balls," he added.

"Aww damn I almost feel bad now, she was really looking for a shoulder to lean on and I pushed her away," I stated, ignoring Derrick's last comment.

"No, no you shouldn't feel bad because everything that happened to her she brought it on herself. Fuck that shit ain't nobody bout to have no pity on her," he replied.

"I mean you right but true enough I was a little cold towards her and man wow. She started talking and I just tuned her out because I..."

"Nigga I know you feeling some kind of way right now but what is with all this

emotionalism? This shit ain't like you," he said, cutting me off.

"I have been a bit sensitive the last two days huh," I recalled.

"Yea nigga you been crying and whining like a bitch since you got here son," Derrick said with a smirk.

"Fuck you nigga," I snapped.

"I plan to before you leave bruh, trust that," he said while flashing that charming smile.

"Whatever, so you think that she'll be back," I inquired, ignoring him once again.

"It is Tyra so... maybe she'll take the hint and stay away, or maybe she won't. You know she was always the hardheaded and stubborn one," he stated as he leaned against the mantle.

"In that case I guess I should be ready for another visit," I laughed.

"Yea well, it's after six and it's Sunday

so if you're still planning on going out we need to make a move ASAP," Derrick warned.

"Oh yea, but I was thinking about going somewhere in the city. There's not a whole lot of variety out here and like you just mentioned things close early," I replied.

"Well either way bro a decision needs to be made so we can coordinate everything," Derrick said.

"Umm ok, let's go to Brennan's in the French quarter. I know parking might be a bitch but they can accommodate us and they're open till either eleven or midnight I think," I stated, finally prying myself off the sofa.

"Ok well is that what you're wearing?" he asked.

"Nah, I'm about to go freshen up and change now," I answered, "If you want, you call the restaurant and see if you can reserve a spot for us," I added.

"Aight let me call Lisa and tell her

what the plan is first and I'll be down here waiting for you," he stated, taking a seat in my dad's old recliner.

"Ok sounds good, I shouldn't be too long, I just need to wash up and brush my teeth," I said as I started up the stairs.

CHAPTER 15: DISCUSSION TABLE

An hour later Derrick, Lisa, and I were at the restaurant waiting to be seated. Since Lisa had invited a guest she left DJ and Malaysia with her mom. I'd kind of hoped they could come but I figured somebody must want to have an adult discussion. Not sure if I was up for it but I was here now and I left the car at the house so I couldn't escape.

"Party of five for St. Julian," a young lady announced.

"Over here," I called, lifting my hand to be seen through the crowd.

"I'm Tamara gain welcome to the

Bourbon House, and if you'd follow me right this way I'll take you to your table," she announced cheerfully.

"Thank you, the other two people in our party will be joining us shortly," Lisa stated as we took our seats.

"Not a problem at all, would you like to order drinks or some appetizers to get you started while you wait," the young lady asked.

"Umm sure I'll take a strawberry lemonade if you have it, and what was your name again," I said.

"Yes we do, and my apology, I'm Tamara, what can I get for you maim," she replied, proceeding to take our drink orders.

"I'll have the same, and he'll have a root beer," Lisa answered.

"Ok great, I'll give you guys a few minutes to look over the menu and get those drinks out right away," Tamara stated.

"One second love, go head and fire two orders of the crab fingers bordelaise and two

orders of BBQ shrimp," I interjected, lightly grabbing Tamara's arm as she turned to leave.

"You sure you just want two orders? Derrick could probably eat two by his self," Lisa laughed.

"Ha, ha very funny Lisa," Derrick smirked.

"You might be right about that instead of the bordelaise give us one oyster platter and one shrimp platter, and do just one order of the BBQ shrimp. You think that'll be good Lisa," I said, passing the decision making to her.

"How about the catfish instead of the oysters? I'm not a fan of them and I doubt they'll be anything left when our guests arrive," she replied.

"Ok that's fine with me," I said.

"So I have one catfish platter, one shrimp platter, BBQ shrimp, two strawberry lemonades, and a root beer," Tamara

confirmed.

"Yep you got it, and could you bring out some small plates so we can all share," I requested.

"Sure, I'll go get your drinks and the food should be out in about fifteen to twenty minutes," she said.

"Thanks, by then the rest of our party should have arrived," Lisa stated.

"Ok I'll be back as soon as I can," Tamara chirped as she walked off.

"So that was a pretty good service today huh," Lisa asked.

"It was great till my uncle got up there with his debacle of a message," I replied with a forced smile.

"Come on Shawn I can read through that fake grin you giving honey and maybe I was wrong for bring that up but..."

"It's cool, seems like Ms. Angel was right," I said, cutting her off.

"Where did you see her," Derrick asked.

"At the church, it was her that stopped me from leaving," I answered.

"Umm Shawn...," Derrick started, "I don't think you saw Ms. Angel at the church today," he stated hesitantly.

"Dude what do you mean, I was talking to her in the lobby," I exclaimed.

"Shawn Ms. Angel died two years ago, I called you myself when it happened," Lisa chimed in, "Don't you remember? You sent a floral and a five hundred dollar gift card to the family," she added.

"Nah... yall I..."

"Hey guys I have your drinks and your appetizers will be out in a bit," Tamara said, as she gave us our drinks.

"Thanks honey, can you let us know when the remainder of our party gets here," Lisa said.

"Sure thing!" Tamara agreed.

"Shawn I don't know who you were talking to but it wasn't Ms. Angel bro," Derrick stated.

"Dude it was her, I don't know how but it was her," I persisted.

"Well I guess you were talking to a ghost then bro, maybe when I get off tomorrow I can take you to her grave, it's not far from your parents tomb," he replied.

"Man I..."

"Don't worry we won't tell anybody," Lisa laughed, "but I think whoever or whatever it was gave you the push you needed," she continued.

"I think so too, plus you said yourself that you felt better after you said what you said," Derrick added.

"Yall are seriously trying to convince me that I was talking to a ghost," I laughed.

"Dude if you don't believe we can

*swing by there tonight after we leave here,"
he said.*

*"Ok, ok I believe you, just... I don't
know. So how did the kids take being left at
home," I asked, changing the subject.*

*"DJ had a fit but Malaysia was
sleeping when you guys came," Lisa said.*

"I figured he would," I replied.

*"Yea well before everybody else gets
here there's something we want to ask you,"
Derrick informed me.*

*"Wait let me guess, you guys are ghosts
too and I just ordered all that food for
myself," I said.*

*"Real funny, but we've been thinking
about it and we think that you would make a
great Padrino for Malaysia and my sister
would be the Madrina," Lisa stated.*

*"Yea you already spoil DJ rotten but
this weekend I've seen you be a real daddy to
him and that kind of sealed the deal for me,
for us to ask you," Derrick added.*

"Wow I don't know what to say," I replied, a little shocked by the request.

"Say yes nigga, we didn't just propose to you," he joked.

"I mean one minute yall telling me I'm looney and the next you're asking me to christen your daughter," I said.

"We didn't call you looney, we just reminded you that the woman that you claimed to have been talking to has been dead for two years," Lisa laughed.

"Well it all sounds the same to me," I pouted.

"Ok well I talked to Bishop Tolbert after church, the ceremony will be held at his church the Sunday after her first birthday, and we expect to see you there," she continued.

"So you're telling me I have three months to make up my mind and get my ass back here," I laughed, "Looks like your guest are here Lisa," I added, noticing the hostess walking toward our table with a couple.

"Looks like our food is ready too," Derrick noted.

"Well hello again everybody, it looks like we got here just in time," Bishop Tolbert announced as he and a gorgeous woman were seated with us.

"I'd say you have perfect timing," I stated.

"Nice to see you smiling brother, but before I get in trouble let me introduce my wife Brittany," he said.

"We met this morning during Sunday school," Lisa replied, reaching over to shake her hand.

"You know it's funny you said that because Sunday school is actually how we met as well," Bishop Tolbert stated, as he removed his jacket.

"Carl I don't think these people are interested in hearing love stories," Brittany said.

"Oh no we don't mind it might be just

the thing we need to hear," Derrick encouraged.

"Absolutely, Derrick and I met in school along with Deshawn and his ex-wife, Tyra," Lisa added.

"Well it's kind of funny because it wasn't actually in a Sunday school class. As you all know Evangelist Angel was our district superintendent but when she passed two years ago we had to find a replacement. Well this young lady here came highly recommended and long story short through us working together in ministry we became partners in life," he explained, also confirming that Ms. Angel had died.

"Wow that's pretty amazing, maybe one day I'll find my good thing," I said, looking around the table.

"In time my brother, in time! I was thirty-six when we met and believe me I was long overdue if you know what I mean," he laughed.

"Carl," Brittany scolded.

"What we're all adults," he said innocently.

"I think you might want to stop while you're ahead," Lisa cautioned.

"Hey guys I apologize, can I get you two something to drink," Tamara stated apologetically, "If you all would like I could take your entrée orders as well," she continued.

"We'll have the lemonade just to make it easy," Bishop Tolbert replied.

"I think we'll need a few more minutes on the entrées," Derrick said.

"Ok I'll get you guys those drinks and some refills for everyone else," Tamara said before dashing off.

Twenty minutes later we were finishing up our apps and were waiting on our entrées. While we waited Bishop Tolbert talked a little more about how he and Michelle got together and keeping a balance between ministry and home. I thought it was pretty interesting for the most part but Michelle didn't seem too happy about him discussing some of the more personal issues. Derrick and Lisa gave their two cents here and there and I just kind of sat there and nibbled as I listened. Since my marriage was a disaster I didn't feel like I had much to say about anything. However, I believe if Tyra had been there she might have been more apt to talking about how this and that went wrong.

"So Shawn do you think you'll ever get remarried?" Bishop Tolbert asked, sensing a slight disconnect.

"Maybe... maybe one day Bishop, but I doubt it'll be anytime soon," I answered.

"I understand that feeling but don't let doubt interfere with God's plan, by the way I heard about the rumors and all and I know what you said earlier, but was that reason for you leaving," he asked.

"Honestly it gave me incentive but no I left because I felt like there wasn't much left for me here. My parents were dead, my marriage was over and here's this opportunity

to see a new place and make six figures a year," I replied.

"Well after talking with your aunt and uncle, I get where the rumors came from and see how things got out of hand. Yet it's been ten years since you've been home? I feel what you're saying but to those who don't know you and only hear what's in the wind it only looks bad for you," he stated.

"Shawn we were here for you the whole time, but you... you kind of shut everybody out and that hurt as friend. We talked a little here and there but we really didn't talk until you had moved and I found out today that I still didn't know everything," Derrick added.

"I didn't mean to make anybody feel any kind of way I was hurting and just wanted to be left alone. If you had reached out to me I wouldn't have turned you away," I said, "Hell you and Lisa were the only family that attended my graduation," I added.

"But you did turn us away, you were answering calls, texts, or anything, then you

moved away," Derrick stated.

"Well in his defense he was mourning and in his eyes he wasn't doing anything wrong, but now I think his eyes have been opened," Bishop Tolbert chimed in.

"Yea I apologize guys, keeping the miscarriage a secret was my wife's decision and I honored that. Now in reference to those rumors the only truth is I am bisexual. I couldn't go into much detail earlier because there were children in the room," I stated, looking around the table.

"You don't have to explain yourself, but like I told you earlier in order to really see the future you've got to let go of the past. I know you have your own relationship with God so there's no need for me to say anything about your lifestyle choices. I'll just encourage you find your foundation again, you might not have liked being dragged to church and all that but I'm sure you've seen the benefits of that now," Bishop Tolbert said.

"I think that's funny how you did the honorable thing by her but she didn't respect

you at all," Lisa interjected.

"Yea but babe I think that just feeds into what Bishop just said. All the churching and things that Shawn's parents taught him molded him into the respectable man we see here today. We make our own decisions and everybody makes a mistake here and there and there's nobody, except Jesus, that can claim to be perfect," Derrick said.

"Well stated, but my question to you Shawn is have you forgiven those people and more importantly have you forgiven yourself," Brittany inquired.

"Like I said earlier, I'm not holding any grudges and I'm working on me because I know things definitely could have been handled differently. Except for the absence of my parents my life is good," I replied.

"Well that a process that you'll have to go through and I know your friends will be there for you every step of the way. I lost my parents the same way you did except I was a teenager. There are still days when I wish I could just talk to my mom or hug my dad but

that's when I lean on God. If my husband is too busy, friends and family can't be reached, I find a corner and just pray. You've been holding on to this for a long time, but I know you can get through it just like I did," Brittany encouraged.

"And so now you see why I love this woman," Bishop Tolbert joked, "but man right here at this table there's a lot of love and people who are willing to go the distance for you. I don't normally give out my number or take many dinner invitations, despite my sexy physique, but I saw something in you and I look forward to hearing from you," he continued.

"Well I'm still mad about being shut out," Derrick pouted before bursting out in laughter.

"Uh huh well the food is here so you won't be mad much longer, and Bishop I'll definitely be in touch," I said as my food was placed in front of me.

"I hope you do man and I also hope it won't be another ten years before we see you

again," Bishop Tolbert joked.

"I promise it won't, Lisa has already made sure of that," I said.

"Boy hush and eat your vegetables," Lisa huffed.

"Plus if I decide to rent the house I'll definitely have to come back periodically to see about my property, unless Derrick wants to keep being my groundskeeper," I laughed.

"I've been doing it for ten years, I don't think ten more would hurt," he stated, before stuffing a spoonful of creole in his mouth.

"Sounds like you have some decisions to make then huh," Brittany asked.

"Yea over the next couple days I'll be meeting with some people to see where I want to go with it," I replied.

"Well Shawn if you need any help I know a real good realtor," she stated with a smile.

"Ok great I'll keep that in mind," I said, finally cutting into my steak.

CHAPTER 16: HARD DECISIONS

It's been two days since the fiasco at the church and the encounter with my ex-wife. However, the day still turned out to be a pretty good day overall. The dinner guest turned out to be pretty interesting too, but it was my last day in the old house and I still had a decision to make about the house. After meeting with a couple realtors and a contractor it was suggested that I just do some updates but I wasn't so keen on changing anything. So I opted to make repairs where they were needed and eventually decide to sell or rent. Even though I wasn't really fond of either idea. If I sold it, it would be a piece of my parent's legacy that I'd never get back, and if I rented it I was taking the chance of letting someone destroy it. Also, since Derrick vouched for her, I reached out to Tyra to see what she had to say. She was supposed to be stopping by at some point, but I wasn't expecting a warm and fuzzy reunion. Still the next day I was going to be on a plane back to D.C. and this chapter of my life would finally be closed. After some more extensive conversation with Bishop I've come to the conclusion that I've been my own roadblock. I've carried the guilt and shame of arguing with my parents just before they died for ten years, plus I had never confronted the rumor mill. So it was time for me to be free.

Around noon, while the housecleaners were cleaning up, one of the workers stumbled up on a key box in my dad's office. With the exception of some old books, files, and decorative items, I thought I had cleared out the most of his personal effects. Obviously I missed something, but now the task was finding the key or some other way to open it. I remembered seeing a small set of keys in the desk when I did my initial sweep but I had no idea where they were now. So I began to settle in on the idea that I'd either have to break it or have the lock professionally opened. In the meantime, I continued overseeing as things were pulled out and packed away. I'd planned to organize it all into categories and then go from there. Some of it would go into storage or be donated to goodwill and the rest would either be taken back to D.C. with me or thrown away. It was a pretty big project I was taking on, but I figured if I could at least get the house cleaned and decluttered it would be a good start. Then when I came back for Malaysia's christening I could get some more done. There were some plumbing and electrical issues I needed to have fixed and I also wanted to update the HVAC. The house itself was pretty sound and as I said before I didn't really want to change anything structural unless I had to.

"Mr. St Julian my crew is finishing up with the downstairs we can get started on the upper level after lunch and then we'll be good," Walter, the site supervisor, said.

"That sounds good, just remember to

stay clear of the master and I'm staying in one of the guest rooms so I'll handle those two myself," I replied.

"Ok great, well it's almost one so we'll take an hour for lunch, be back here for two, and hopefully be finished by four. If upstairs is like the main level we'll probably be done before then," he informed me.

"Good deal man, I'll see you guys when you get back," I said.

"In the meantime I can keep looking for keys in that office if you'd like," Walter offered.

"Sure that would be great, make sure you guys lock the door behind you," I stated before walking off.

Within maybe twenty minutes or so the cleaning crew had cleared out and I was alone. I figured we probably wouldn't find that key so I took the box and put it in the room I was using. After securing it in my bag I decided to get started on my parent's room. If I could have worn some of my dad's clothes they definitely would have been coming home with me but they'd need some serious alterations. My dad was around 5'9 and weighed almost three hundred pounds, something we'd had numerous conversations about. I'd try and get him to go to the gym with me or show him and my mom healthier ways to eat, but it was a lost cause. Those two were set in their ways and there was no changing their minds. As I went through the closet I did see some belts, ties, hats, and other accessories that I would definitely be taking home. My dad might have been a thick guy but he was always dressed clean and smelled nice. Two of the biggest attributes I can say I got from him. My mom taught me some fashion tips too but it was my dad that I often caught myself emulating. Many times I would call myself Daniel 2.0 since I had his looks and sense of style, but I was taller and muscular. He hated that yet I knew deep down he was proud of me and the man I was becoming. That's probably the reason why he said some of the things he said that night, not to hurt me but because of pride. Anyway, I got about halfway through the closet and I realized I really might have bitten off more than I could chew. Since I never really came into my parents room I never realized how big the closets were, plus there was a chest and two nightstands that I still needed to work through. Thankfully they sprung for a nice system so both of them were well organized. My mom's closet would be a breeze since there was obviously nothing I could do with any of her clothes. Though there was a white, full-length fur coat that I might be able to pass with. My dad had a few nice coats too but I would have to get them taken in to fit. I decided to throw away all of his underwear except the ones that were still in the packages. Those I would give to goodwill along with the suits and shoes I couldn't wear. Then just as I had finished picking out the things I wanted to keep for myself I heard the doorbell followed by a knock. I figured it was the crew coming back so I rushed down to answer. To my surprise it was Tyra and this time she wasn't alone.

"So can we come in or you still don't want me in the house," she stated, clutching

the child's hand while she looked me over.

"Uh yea sure... come in..." I said hesitantly as I stepped aside.

"So..."

"Let's just get straight to the point Tyra, who's the kid and what was so important for you to tell me Sunday?" I interrupted, cutting off the small talk before it got started.

"Damn ok, well this is my son, Jason," Tyra replied, beckoning for the child to shake my hand, "and he was part of what I wanted to tell you about," she continued.

"Part of it, so what's the other news besides my aunt making your sins front page news," I inquired.

"Well... I guess there's no easy way to say this. Things haven't really been good for me since we separated, his father got arrested, and your aunt with her shenanigans, and the man we're staying with now..."

"He hits us all the time, especially

mommy," the young child, no older than six or seven blurted out as Tyra struggled to speak.

"What do you mean he hits yall lil man," I probed, looking directly into his eyes.

"He doesn't like me too much because mommy had me with another man and he..."

"That's enough Jason, why don't you go outside and play so Mr. Deshawn and I can talk, but stay by the window so I can see you," Tyra scolded.

"But mom..."

"Jason I said go outside and play," she retorted.

"Ok," he agreed.

"Tyra are you being abused," I asked once the boy was outside.

"He doesn't abuse me he just gets mad sometimes when things aren't right and..."

"No, no I'm not going to stand here and listen to you make excuses for this dude.

I'd rather that boy out there tell me what's going on than for you to try and cover up the truth. You forget I know you Tyra," I stated cutting her off again.

"Ok, ok yes he beats me and sometimes he abuses my son, but if I leave we'll have nowhere to go. We'll be homeless," she replied, lowering her eyes to the floor.

"Homeless, don't you work? What about your family? Isn't there somebody you could go to," I asked.

"He made me quit my job and my mom and aunt haven't really talked to me since the mess started with Penny and then when I started talking to Gerald they really cut me off, and I'm scared that if I run he might come afte

r us" she said, her eyes filling with tears.

"So this dude can kill you and nobody would look for you because you've alienated yourself from them and I bet if that boy's father knew what was happening he wouldn't

be happy either. I mean I don't know what to tell you, I'm not about to give you any money or get involved with you and dude," I said sternly, taking a seat across from her.

"So what am I supposed to do," she cried as the tears began to flow.

"I don't know Tyra, but it doesn't really seem like you're ready to do anything. It's more like you just came over to pull an empathy card and get a handout, but I'm leaving tomorrow and outside of this house and my friends I have no attachments here. What I will do for you is make some phone calls and hopefully we can get you some help," I stated just as the doorbell rang.

"Shawn I'm sorry for what happened between us, and I appreciate anything you can do for my son and I, please take my mom's number and give her a call. Let her know what's going on and where I'm at," she pleaded as she got up, wiped her face, and handed me a folded piece of paper, "She always liked you so maybe she'll talk to you," she added.

"You sound like you've given up, and that doesn't like the woman I know, but before you throw in the towel you think about that child out there. Every day you open your eyes you pray for strength and you fight for him. I'll do what I can but Tyra you've got to want this to end before it gets better," I attempted to encourage.

"Thanks Shawn," she said as she went out the door.

"Hey Mr. St. Julian I was just about to call you," Walter shouted from the sidewalk.

"Oh I'm here you guys can go on back in now, my guest and I were just wrapping some things up," I yelled back as I escorted Tyra down the steps.

"Come on Jason," Tyra called out, reaching her hand for him.

"I hope we didn't interrupt anything," Walter said when he got closer to me.

"Nah man that's just my ex-wife and her son," I said nonchalantly.

"Ok no need for explanation there, I'll get the crew back on the job and we should be out of your hair in about an hour or so," he replied.

"Oh nah man, I've been gone for ten years and you can see that boy is no more than five or six, maybe seven at the most," I laughed.

"Ok got you, every time my ex comes around it's for money or something for the kids. Usually not a pretty scene," Walter laughed.

"Well thankfully I don't have that trouble, we split before kids came into the picture, but listen I won't hold you guys from working and I'll get back to this bedroom. Speaking of getting back to work, you wouldn't have a few boxes you can spare huh," I asked.

"Yea sure let me get the guys going and I'll bring some up to you in a bit," he answered.

"Great, thanks man," I said.

In no less than maybe an hour and a half all the packing was done. Now I had the task of getting everything to where it was supposed to go. I thought about stuffing some boxes in the truck of the car before the mover came to pick it up, but that might not work well. I also didn't have the heart to really throw anything away so everything that wasn't going to storage or D.C. would be donated. Derrick was supposed to be coming to help me, but there really wasn't much left to do. The movers were coming at five to get the car and things that were going to D.C. and goodwill would be here shortly to pick the donations. All Derrick and I had to do was take the rest to storage. I was leaving the furniture in place for staging if we got to that point so we should have an easy job. If it hadn't been for Walter and his crew of cleaners and packers, I would probably still be scrabbling to get everything done. So while I waited for the pickups I went ahead and made those phone calls I promised I would make. I couldn't believe the situation Tyra had gotten herself into but all we could do now was pray that things got better. Despite my muscles I was no superman and frankly I didn't think it was my place to get tangled up in that. However, I did feel bad for them so I was keeping my word.

CHAPTER 17: CHAPTER CLOSED

It was about a quarter after five when Derrick pulled up in the driveway. Goodwill had already came and the movers where hitching the car to the truck. I'd had a nice conversation with Tyra's mom and a hear full to tell Derrick once he got in the house.

"So you bout ready to head back to D.C. huh," he asked as he came up the steps.

"Yes and no, but you don't look like you ready to work," I replied.

"What you mean work," Derrick shrieked.

"Son we still got to bring the rest of

those boxes in there to storage and you looking all blue collar with your shirt and tie," I said, pretending to fix his tie.

"Aww man it ain't nothing to move a few boxes and this can come off easy son," he stated, swatting my hand away and loosening the tie knot.

"Ok well get on in here and let's get this started. Oh and you'll never guess who came by today," I said.

"She came back huh," Derrick laughed, following me inside.

"Yea she did and she had another story to tell me, but she didn't come alone, this time she brought a kid with her," I told him.

"Oh was it Jason?" he asked.

"Yea she said the father is locked up," I answered.

"He is got ten years for drug trafficking," he informed me.

"Oh wow, so at least that part is true,"

I said, "She also told me about this dude Gerald that she's with now and how's he's been mistreating her and the kid," I continued.

"Gerald who? Not the Omega from UNO huh?" Derrick inquired.

"I'm not sure who he is she just told me his name was Gerald and she seemed scared of him, but I'm like why you coming to me," I stated making my way up to my room.

"Maybe she still feels safe with you," he suggested.

"I can get that... maybe, but still what do you expect me to do about it. Like I told her I'm leaving tomorrow and I'm not giving anybody any money," I exclaimed.

"So you think she might be trying to get away from this guy? If you're talking about who I think you are dude is bad news and he's the one Jason's father was running for when he got caught," Derrick explained.

"Wait, wait, wait you're telling me that

Tyra has gotten herself tangled up with some drug lord who also happens to be a hot tempered domestic offender," I cried, getting more and more concerned for her by the minute.

"Hot tempered is right, but Shawn calm down," he said.

"Calm down, how can you stand there and tell me to calm down when my ex-wife could be getting her brains knocked out as we speak," I snapped.

"Dude listen to me, he might shake her up a bit but I doubt he'll do anything drastic. The police have eyes on him nearly twenty-four seven," Derrick said trying to assure me.

"The police have eyes on him but he's still doing his thing and who's to say that he couldn't get one of his goons to do the job. I mean shit there's nothing I can really do beyond what I've done but now I'm really concerned for her and even more so for Jason," I replied.

"I understand, but look if it makes you

feel any better Lisa and I will try and keep tabs on her too. I might be able to pull some strings and Lisa knows a couple ladies that work with battered women," he stated.

"I mean like I said, I've done what I can, but I just don't know how I'd feel if something happened to them," I said.

"All you can do is pray and let God handle it. I get that you're concerned but you aren't responsible for the decisions that she's made since you guys separated," Derrick stated, "You really are an awesome guy dude," he added.

"Yea I guess, so let's go head and get moving so we can get these boxes to the storage before they close," I said while looking through my bag for a pair of shorts or sweats for Derrick.

"Mr. St. Julian we're all ready to go, I just need you to sign a few forms before we hit the road," one of the movers called from downstairs.

"Ok great I'll be down in a few," I

shouted back.

"Hey Shawn what's this," Derrick asked, noticing the key box I'd placed on the bed.

"Oh one of the guys found that in my dad's office earlier but there's no key for it," I replied.

"Oh ok, so what you going to do with it," he asked.

"Got to get it open somehow," I laughed, "but let me go tend to these movers and then we can roll," I added, handing him a pair of shorts.

"Ok, you mind if I try something while you're gone," he asked.

"Uh sure," I said as I walked out of the door.

Thirty minutes later we were on our way to the storage unit. When we got there it was almost like a ghost town. I figured if it was like that all the time I wouldn't have much to worry even though the security system was pretty old and antiquated. The attendant at the front desk seemed a little flirty, but neither of us are into cougars. We made quick work of getting the boxes into the unit and made our way back to the house. Seeing Derrick in a wife beater and shorts with dress socks and loafers on was kind of funny but sexy at the same time. I caught myself gazing at his dick a few times, imagining it in my mouth. I'd been craving it all weekend but the opportunity for a one on one session never presented itself. The thirst was real and it was only intensified by the events of Friday night. First the teasing then the threesome with Lisa. I had to taste and feel that dick before I went home.

"So you ready to finish what we started," Derrick asked.

"Huh," I replied, confused by the randomness of his question.

"I see how you keep looking at me and I haven't forgot about our unfinished business," he stated as he licked his lips.

"Unfinished business, you mean you

want to tease me some more," I laughed, looking away from him.

"Nah ain't gon be no teasing my nigga. Matter of fact you started that shit when I picked you up from the airport Friday," he answered.

"Ha, nah nigga I recall somebody else being real touchy feely but when I felt on them back they started getting all nervous and shit," I continued to laugh, still focusing my attention outside the window.

"I was only checking you out but you just pulled my dick out and started sucking it," he countered.

"Like you want me to do now huh," I shot back, briefly glancing over at him.

"I know it's on your mind," he said confidently.

"You do huh," I laughed.

"You laughing now, but wait till I get you to that house," he warned.

"You said that before and nothing happened," I retorted.

"Ok you gon see," he stated.

"I'm sure I will," I said in disbelief, knowing full well that I was more than ready to find out.

Ten minutes later we were pulling back into my parent's driveway. The rest of the drive had been quiet but the anticipation of what was next was blasting. When we got up the steps I noticed that there was a note taped to the door. Curiously I yanked it down and once inside I unfolded it to reveal its contents. Anxiously Derrick kept asking me who it was from and what it said, but as I proceeded to read I just tuned him out. It seemed that while we were gone I'd had a visitor and since she missed me she left a note expressing her thoughts about me. I was honestly surprised, but at the same time I felt like everything was complete now. In the rather lengthy note was an apology from my Aunt Penny. First for the drama during my marriage and the rumors that she spread. Then for the scene she caused at the gas station Saturday night and embarrassment Sunday morning. She also went on to say that she was proud of the way I carried myself amidst all I've been through. Then there was a lot of fluff about how we're family and we needed to support each other and blah, blah, blah. Finally to end it she left a phone number and asked that I call sometimes. I guess Bishop Tolbert's conversation with them is what prompted the visit but then maybe she wasn't so bad after all.

"So are going to call her," Derrick asked after I explained it to him.

"I will, probably after I get back to D.C. though," I answered, "After all these years she probably just felt bad about what she did. They made up all those rumors to hurt me but I still rose up," I continued.

"I can agree with that, but umm Shawn, I thought about what you said earlier. There's a little key attached to the ring you gave me you think it might work on the box?" he asked.

"It's worth a try," I said.

"Ok and you might as well come up on out of them clothes because we still have some business to take care of my nigga," Derrick stated, trailing real close behind me as we went up the stairs.

"Yea ok, get off me nigga," I said shrugging him off as we reached the top.

"Oh it's get off you now huh," he laughed, "You acted like I was just talking shit son, but I'm about to show you ass," he added, peeling off his shirt.

"Ok nigga, give that key so I can see if it works," I replied, trying my hardest to ignore how sexy he was at that moment.

"There you go, you see what's up with that and I'm a check this out back here," he said, tossing the key onto the bed and simultaneously pulling down my pants and boxers.

"Oh shit," I shrieked when I felt his tongue glide across my hole, "Oh fuck, fuck,

fuck, Derrick it... chill out a minute bruh," I *snapped reluctantly.*

"What's wrong yo," he asked.

"Ain't nothing wrong that shit feel good and I can't focus, plus the key worked," I said.

"Oh damn, so what's in the box," he inquired anxiously.

"Shit I'm trying to see now," I replied.

"Well while you figure that out I'm a go back to what I was doing," Derrick said before slithering his tongue back into my hole.

"You so damn nasty nigga," I laughed.

"You like that shit though don't you," he asked.

"I ain't answering that," I hissed, trying to compose myself.

"You just did my nigga," Derrick laughed, slapping my ass with his hard dick.

"So this the pistol whipping I was

supposed to be getting," I snapped.

"Oh I ain't got started yet son," he stated as he spit lubed his dick.

"Yo nigga you not about to ram that big ass muthafucka in me dry," I cried, pushing away from him.

"Ain't nothing dry about this back here my nigga," he said, ignoring my words as he pushed the head of his dick inside me.

"Mumm shit... let me get in a better position yo," I moaned, putting my knees up on the bed.

"Damn this shit tight and wet as fuck nigga," he groaned, pushing all ten, thick inches inside me.

For the next twenty minutes Derrick pounded my cakes doggy style. All I could do was grab a pillow and bite down on it to muffle my moans. Derrick tried to take it from me so he could hear me scream, but I wasn't letting go. I could tell I was getting wetter by the stroke and my dick was throbbing indicating that I was about to cum. As much as I'd played hard to get I was loving every moment of it and Derrick knew just how I wanted it. After a good workout from the back he turned me over on my back and grinded that dick deep inside me till we both came. I'll admit our quickie wasn't the grand reunion sex that we both wanted, but Lisa was expecting us for dinner. So it seemed I'd have to wait till I returned for a refill or maybe we could get in another quickie after dinner. In other news the box was open, however since Derrick insisted on proving his point I hadn't had a chance to examine its contents.

"So you almost ready to go bro, you know how Lisa is," Derrick called from the bedroom.

"Yea I'll be out in a minute," I yelled.

"You know you could have just washed up at the house," he stated.

"And have Lisa smell sex on me," I joked as I stepped into the bedroom.

"If that's the case maybe I should have

showered too," Derrick laughed.

"Nah then you'd be too fresh for just having moved a few boxes," I said.

"Yea you're right, too risky, but I will try and get a quick one in before we eat," he replied.

"Well just don't move too fast and give anything away, but... I think I've got everything, you ready," I stated.

"Everything except some clothes on yo naked ass, you must really want all of Violet to be talking about yo ass," he laughed.

"They've talked before," I laughed.

When we arrived at Derrick and Lisa's DJ was plowing out the door before we could park. As he came down the steps I could hear him yelling, "Padrino, Padrino...," over and over. The excitement in his eyes was priceless, but Derrick seemed a little annoyed. I guess from a parent's perspective it's dangerous for him to be running out to the car like he did, but how could you be mad at someone so adorable. Not to mention it felt good to have a welcome committee, even if it was just one person.

"Padrino! I missed you," DJ exclaimed, almost literally jumping into my arms.

"What about me son," Derrick asked.

"I missed you too Daddy, but come on the food is almost ready," DJ cried, rushing us into the house.

"Ok, ok we're coming, let us get Padrino's stuff out the truck," Derrick said.

"Hey lil man, why don't you run inside and tell your mom I have a surprise for her," I stated, "Derrick you don't have to take all that stuff out, just the bag with my clothes and the box needs to come inside," I continued, turning my attention to Derrick.

"Oh you know what I wasn't even thinking about that, but what about this surprise you have," he asked.

"It's in the box I put behind the seat," I

replied, grabbing my overnight bag and the box leaving Derrick to put back the other stuff he took out.

"Shawn what's this talk about a surprise," Lisa inquired, meeting me at door with DJ clinging to her hip.

"I got it right here," I said with a smile.

"Well give it to me nigga," she snapped.

"Hold on, let's go inside and wait for Derrick," I laughed, taking a step back from her.

"Derrick hurry up I don't want my food to get cold," she yelled.

"I'm right here babe," Derrick panted as he hopped up the steps.

"Damn girl you trying to make me stay," I laughed, looking over at the spread she had on the table.

"That depends on this surprise you

have for me," Lisa countered, grabbing the box from my arm.

"Mommy, mommy I want to see," DJ sang excitedly.

"OH MY GOD!" Lisa squealed as she opened the box.

"Oww that's pretty mommy," DJ said.

"Shawn are you serious? You're really giving this to me," Lisa asked as she pulled the surprise out of the box.

"Yea why not," I laughed.

"This was your moms wasn't it," she continued to question.

"Yes and now it's yours, I left some other stuff in the closet that you might want too. Derrick still has his key so you guys can go over there whenever you get ready," I said.

"Wow I'm almost speechless," she stated, "but yall come on and eat this food before it gets cold," she added.

After dinner we all sat around the table

looking at each other, too stuffed to move.
Lisa had really outdone herself this time.
There was fried chicken, mashed potatoes,
meatballs, cornbread, sweet peas, rice
dressing, macaroni and cheese, strawberry
shortcake, and more of those pineapple
empanadas. I think I ate till I couldn't feel my
jaws anymore. When we were finally able to
move, DJ was sent to his room to finish
homework and get ready for bed. Malaysia
was already sleep so Lisa took her upstairs as
well, leaving Derrick and I at the table. I
suggested that it was a good time for him to
go take that shower, and while he was doing
that I would check out the key box. So he went
upstairs and I grabbed my bag from the den
and made my way down to the basement suite.
When I got to the room I threw the bag on the
bed and took a minute to think about where
I'd put the key. Then I remembered it was still
on Derrick's keyring with the house key I'd
given him. So I ran back up the stairs and
grabbed his keys.

"Calling it a night already Shawn,"
Lisa asked as she came down the stairs.

"No not yet, I just wanted to move my stuff out of the den," I replied.

"Oh ok, well if you need anything I'll be up here cleaning. Derrick's in the shower but he should be back down shortly," she said.

"Ok cool, once I sort through this box I'll be back or maybe yall can come down," I suggested.

"Doesn't matter, let's just say whoever finishes first goes to the other, and thank you Shawn," Lisa said with a smile.

"Don't mention it, I figured you'd get more use out of it than me and I didn't want to give all her stuff to goodwill," I replied.

"Still I know they both meant a lot to you so thanks again, now I better get to these dishes before the itis sets in," she laughed.

Few minutes later I was back down in the basement getting ready to open the box for the second time. From what I saw the first time it was mostly old papers, but why lock them away. There had to be something important about the contents of that box and I was about to find out. So I made myself comfortable, turned the key, and proceeded to check it out. As I examined the papers I realized they were all mostly legal documents. Such as a copy of both my parents wills, power of attorney, deeds to the house, etc., however, there were two things that caught my attention. There was a bank deposit log to for a bank account I never knew about and a key obviously for a safe deposit box at the same bank. As I continued to sift through the box I found an envelope addressed to my mom and I. Curious and anxious I quickly opened it and found a handwritten letter from my dad that had been written no more than a couple weeks before he died. As I began to read it his words confirmed my findings and there was in fact a secret account that he had been keeping since I was a baby. The key was to a safe deposit box located at Regions bank where he'd stashed some other values that may prove useful in the event that something happened to him.

So here I was all ready to go and there was still some unfinished business I needed to handle. Maybe if I'd gotten the box open earlier I could have gone to the bank today and seen what was what. Considering that this account had been in effect since I was one or two years old and the frequency and amount of the deposits made I was looking at a nice unexpected inheritance. Thankfully I had death certificates and all with me and me and my mom's names were on the account according to the paperwork I found. Derrick was already going in to work late tomorrow so he could take me to the airport, so I'd just ask him to leave earlier so we could take care of this before I left. Which is what I explained to him and Lisa when they came down. When they asked me what I would do with the money I told them I was going to transfer it all to my savings account like I'd done with the rest of my parents assets. I also informed them that I'd been thinking about starting a college fund for DJ and Malaysia. If I gave them five thousand a piece and deposited five hundred more each month that would be a little over fifty grand for DJ and almost twice as much for Malaysia. That wasn't even considering any contributions or plans they had already made. So at this point we could consider the kids educations paid in full. Tomorrow at noon I would be leaving Violet for the second time but on a much happier note. I'd settled beefs and come to grips with the guilt and grief I was feeling. I hadn't made a concrete decision on the house but I would be making repairs and doing minor renovations on it over the next year. Then lastly in those moments of solidary after dinner that night I prayed and realized Derrick was right. Tyra's situation was completely out of my hands. So I would be leaving my hometown of Violet, LA with a clear mind and this would be a long awaited close to the worst chapter of my life.